She felt his strong arms lift her to his saddle.

"Hold tight," warned Tom. He wheeled his horse around and took off at full gallop. The four horsemen, pounding behind, were clearly gaining on them.

Forgetful of her dignity, Arabella clung tightly to Tom's jacket, her face pressed into his chest.

After what seemed an eternity, the shouting died away and she could hear only the wind whistling by and the drum of the horse's hooves. Pressed so close against Tom that she could feel his heart beating, she felt perfectly secure. Fancifully, she imagined that this must be how the ladies of the ballads felt, as they galloped off across the saddle bows of their lovers.

She flushed, suddenly embarrassed at the idea, and pulled herself a little away from Tom.

But his arm tightened around her, drawing her close again.

DANGER IN THE WIND
was originally published by Hurst & Blackett, Ltd.

Margaret Eastvale

DANGER IN THE WIND

(Original British title: *Feathers in the Wind*)

PUBLISHED BY POCKET BOOKS NEW YORK

DANGER IN THE WIND

Hurst & Blackett edition published 1973

POCKET BOOK edition published December, 1974

Standard Book Number: 671-77786-6.
This POCKET BOOK edition is published by arrangement with Hurst & Blackett Limited. Copyright, ©, 1973, by Margaret Eastvale. All rights reserved. DANGER IN THE WIND was first published in England under the title: *Feathers in the Wind*. This book, or portions thereof, may not be reproduced by any means without permission of the original publisher: Hurst & Blackett Limited, 3 Fitzroy Square, London W. 1, England.
Front cover illustration by Lou Marchetti.
Printed in the U.S.A.

DANGER
IN THE WIND

1

Arabella stared hopelessly into the clammy white mist. Her eyes ached with the effort of straining to distinguish anything in the hazy whiteness. She shivered and drew the thick folds of the sea cloak more tightly around her. It smelled damp and musty but at least it kept out the worst of the cold.

It had not been the brightest of June days when they left home but she had certainly not imagined that it would turn so chill. Nor that the mist would so swiftly engulf them. It had seemed to swallow them up, totally hiding from them any familiar landmark. They and the boat floated alone in a sea of whiteness.

"Where do you think we are now?" She tried to make it casual but the faintest tremor betrayed her anxiety.

Even Edward at the tiller was blurred in the mist. Then a sudden gust of wind shifted a few wisps of the feathery white vapor and she saw him clearly, his face pale and apprehensive. The mist swirled back. Its eerie whiteness surrounded him as if trying to push its barrier between the only two living creatures in this white world.

Edward's voice sounded strange, as if muffled by the mist.

"I'm not sure, Bella. We must have drifted fairly far along the coast. How long is it since we passed Shoreham?"

Arabella shrugged then realized that he would not see the action through the mist.

"I don't know. Half an hour? Perhaps more. We'll just have to sit it out till this mist lifts. It can't last for ever. Probably it'll disappear as swiftly as it came."

She forced more optimism into her voice than she really felt. Edward was not easily fooled. Gloomily he asked:

7

"When do you think they'll miss us at home?"

"Not till dinner, but what could they do? Only Sam's wife knows we've sailed and anyway, no one could find us till this wretched mist lifts."

Now that revealing wobble crept into Edward's voice. "Father'll be furious!"

"Never mind. It'll be me he blames, not you." Arabella spoke without bitterness, accustomed by now to collecting the blame for anything that offended her brother Joseph. The only son of her father's first marriage, Joseph was old enough to be Arabella's father and was a far stricter guardian than either of her doting parents had ever been.

"That's not fair. It was my idea not yours. I'll tell him so."

"Don't bother. It won't make a pennyworth of difference. He'll say that I'm older than you and should be more responsible. That I should have stopped you." Her voice sharpened in exasperation, partly directed at Edward, more at herself. "He's right too. I can't think what possessed me to agree to your harebrained scheme."

"You should have put your foot down, Aunt dear." There was a gurgle of mirth behind Edward's meek tones.

Arabella chuckled too at the familiar joke. She was relieved to hear the scared note disappear from Edward's voice. Still, however much he mocked, she knew that Joseph would indeed consider her the more to blame.

Perhaps justly, she reflected ruefully. Those two years between fifteen and seventeen did make a vast difference. Not to mention—though Joseph undoubtedly would—that as a female she ought to conduct herself more sensibly.

Was it Joseph's constant carping criticism that drove her to these defiant escapades, she wondered. Or just the screaming boredom of life with Joseph and Sarah and their pudding faced brood. Edward was the only one with any spirit. In him she recognized the spark of impish fun that had characterized his grandfather—Arabella's father. No wonder that she encouraged Edward to run counter to his own father's wishes. Joseph—who certainly had not inherited it—would have quenched that spark, if he could, in Edward or herself.

The sea trip that day had been a bid to escape for a few hours. Even the mist might have been an added adventure to be relished—if she were not so concerned for their safety. If only she did not remember so clearly the bodies recovered from that awful wreck a couple of years ago. She had seen them laid out on the hillside, more than a hundred, before they were placed in their communal grave. The *Brazen* had sunk in a storm but who knew what might happen to Edward's small boat in this hateful obscurity.

She shuddered and exclaimed remorsefully:

"I should have stopped you when I knew Sam wasn't there to take us out. Why didn't we wait for him? He'd have known what to do."

Edward's voice held a puzzled note.

"That was a rum business. Didn't you think his wife sounded odd? She said he'd been called away but wouldn't tell me where, or when he'd be back. And he knew I'd intended to go out today."

"Perhaps he thought your father would prevent you."

Arabella had no doubt that Joseph would have put his foot down had he realized that his son was foolish enough to consider taking a boat to sea in the present crisis. Joseph took the invasion threat very seriously. Even last month, with gales blowing straight into the French coast, he had expected to see the enemy fleet sailing up the channel. He firmly believed that Bonaparte, the arch fiend, would not be bound by natural limitations.

Undoubtedly Joseph would have banned the use of the boat if he had imagined them capable of putting to sea at such a time. But imagination was never Joseph's strong point. Nor could he comprehend that his eldest son thrived on danger.

From a small child Edward had been desperate to follow his grandfather's example and join the Navy. His grandfather had done everything to encourage the ambition. Joseph had fought hard but he was no match for the sea-mad pair.

Everything had been prepared for Edward to join his grandfather's vessel as a midshipman—he would have been aboard her right now—only before the plans could be finalized, Arabella's father had been killed in the bloody carnage at Copenhagen.

Nelson himself had sent a personal letter of sympathy. Captain Ridware, he declared, had given valiant support before he was unluckily shot down. His family were proud but sorrowed the more at his loss.

His father's death confirmed all Joseph's worst fears and despite Edward's pleas the plans were abandoned for his entry into the Navy. It had been a bitter blow in peacetime. Now with the Navy crying out for men to help withstand the threat of French invasion, Edward fretted and chafed at his father's decision.

The boat had been intended as a sop to sweeten the refusal. Joseph had bought it during the short peace hoping that it would satisfy his son's craving for the sea.

Privately, Arabella considered that it only whetted his appetite but she knew better than to tell Joseph so. They had never really got along well. With her father away at sea so often, Arabella had been forced to spend most of her life under Joseph's care. That had been irksome but at least when her father was home she got some respite. Now that Joseph was her official guardian, the clash of temperaments was more bitter. For her mother's sake she tried to keep a still tongue and conform to Joseph's antiquated notions of female behavior, but good resolutions had a habit of wavering.

But, for once, over this matter she had kept out of the argument, managed to restrain herself from adding her persuasions to Edward's. If anything could make Joseph more stubborn against Edward's becoming a sailor, it would be to realize that Arabella was in favor of it.

While all these thoughts churned in her brain, she continued to peer into the blank whiteness. Eyes were useless. Her ears, strained to the uttermost to compensate, caught a fresh sound. Could it be the gentle splash of another boat?

"When do you reckon . . ." Edward's voice broke her concentration and she interrupted him sharply.

"Quiet! I thought I heard something just then."

They both sat silent, ears and eyes vainly striving to penetrate the enshrouding blankness. Edward was the first to break the silence.

"You imagined it."

"No. I'm sure that I heard a boat."

"Probably just a fish jumping."

Arabella shook her head obstinately.

"It was a boat. I'm positive. Listen! There it is again."

This time they both heard the unmistakable ripple and creak.

"By George, you're right, Bella. If we both shout together we can hail them."

Even as he opened his mouth, a terrifying thought struck Arabella.

"No, Edward! Don't call. Suppose it should be the French."

"The French so near our coast? Don't be ridiculous, Bella!" Edward spoke scornfully but she noticed that, all the same, he did not shout. Fearfully she whispered:

"Everyone says that Boney is just waiting for a good sea mist like this to invade us."

"You've been listening to Father's gloomy tales for too long. The French will never come."

Edward's words were valiant but Arabella fancied that she could detect a slight note of doubt. In spite of a fervent wish that he should be right, she could not help objecting:

"They say he has rafts a mile long all ready to put to sea."

Edward snorted:

"What utter rubbish! As if anyone could control a craft that big. Anyway it's much too rough for any raft today. They'd need a flat calm. This isn't the French."

For all his confident assertions, somehow neither of them dared to risk attracting the attention of the unknown vessel.

All the nursery tales of French treachery and Bonaparte's wickedness pounded uncomfortably through Arabella's head. She tried not to remember the gruesome posters portraying in gory detail the anticipated results of a French invasion.

She and Edward could expect little mercy if this were indeed Bonaparte's forces. Better to drown peacefully than risk falling into the hands of the bloodthirsty French.

For what seemed an eternity, she clutched at Edward in petrified silence, praying the unknown boat would pass unsuspecting by.

Suddenly a huge dark shape loomed up. Already it was too close for them to do anything but wait dumbly for the inevitable collision. It came with a slow grinding crash that nearly shook them off their feet.

A bearded figure leaned over the rails of the strange boat and peered down at them.

"Who's there?" came a gruffly suspicious voice.

Dizzy with relief, Arabella let out the breath she had been holding tightly in. Equal relief was evident in Edward's heartfelt:

"Thank God! You're English."

"English?" the great red face split up into creases and the sailor's huge stomach quivered with mirth, "Who d'ye think I was? Boney come to fetch a pair of naughty lads?"

Another, taller figure loomed up behind him.

"Any damage?"

"None to us but it looks like we've made a tidy mess of these lads' boat."

Edward gloomily surveyed the splintering crack through which water oozed ever more swiftly. He looked up at the two men.

"We're shipping water fast. I doubt we'd make land even if we knew our way. Can you take us ashore please?"

Indignantly, Arabella registered the faintest pause before the tall newcomer replied.

"I suppose we must. Come aboard the pair of you. Make their boat fast alongside, Jack."

Arabella furiously resented the unwilling note in his voice but with water lapping round her ankles, this was no time for a haughty refusal. Even this grudging aid was preferable to none.

Edward managed easily to clamber up into the other

ship. Bulky skirts and her overlarge cloak made the process considerably more awkward for Arabella. She was glad that the poor visibility masked her undignified position from the ungracious watchers.

Edward turned to help her but was brushed aside by the taller of their rescuers.

"Look lively, lad! No need to make such heavy weather of it."

He stretched out an irritated arm and dragged Arabella aboard. As, indignantly smoothing down her ruffled petticoats, she glared at him, he realized his error.

"I beg your pardon, Ma'am."

The words were apologetic but the bright twinkle in his slate grey eyes betrayed that he was laughing at her. She stared stiffly past him.

"Best take them below, Tom," The gruff voice came warningly and the taller figure nodded.

"If you'll come this way there's a cabin where you can bide." His voice bore only a trace of the Sussex accent that characterized his stout companion's speech. Arabella was hard put to place Tom. He had that indefinable air of command yet he was dressed in as rough a garb as his comrade.

Still, whoever he was, she had not forgiven him for laughing at her.

"Thank you, but I prefer to stay on deck," she stated in her iciest tones.

Annoyingly he was totally unruffled.

"Maybe, but it's more convenient to have you below."

His companion's voice came more urgently:

"Quickly, Tom, the men aren't happy about this daylight run. They'll be worse if they find out there's a wench aboard. That's always accounted ill luck."

With a very poor grace, Arabella allowed herself to be led to the companionway. The ship was not as vast as its dramatic appearance had suggested. Through the mist she caught glimpses of the crew. To her astonishment, any sailors they encountered moved quickly out of her path, faces averted.

Only the man at the wheel kept his post. Something

about his thickset figure struck her as familiar. Impulsively she exclaimed:

"Edward, look. Isn't that Sam?"

Her clear voice carried to the man and he turned a startled face in their direction. Triumphantly, Arabella declared:

"It is! Sam! What are you doing here?"

The bearded sailor gripped her elbow painfully.

"No questions, Miss, please."

She stared in open-mouthed astonishment at him.

"But it is Sam. Our boatman. Why can't I speak to him?"

Edward shook his head slightly and frowned to reinforce the warning. Puzzled she fell silent. The stout sailor stayed only to see them safely into the cabin.

Arabella sank down on to one of the bunks and raised perplexed green eyes to Edward.

"What is going on here? Why won't they let me speak to Sam?"

Edward grinned faintly.

"I had the strong impression that Sam wasn't keen to speak to us."

"But why? What's the mystery?"

Edward shrugged his slim shoulders.

"I'm not sure but I imagine we've run into a bunch of smugglers."

"Smugglers!" Horror made Arabella's voice shriller than she intended.

"Hush, Bella. They'll hear you."

Round-eyed, Arabella stared at him. Excitement had heightened his color, his eyes glowed. Edward was enjoying their adventure. After a moment of pure exasperation, her sense of humor resurfaced.

"Well I suppose that smugglers are better than the French—just!"

"That's gratifying to hear."

She swung around to discover that the tall sailor, Tom, had returned. Laughter lines creased his eyes as he grinned down at her. She reddened and looked away.

The mocking note was intensified as he turned to Edward.

"Is your sister always this sulky?"

With an angry gasp, Arabella rose to the full dignity of her five foot nothing:

"I am not his sister. I'm his aunt."

Tom raised an amused eyebrow.

"No wonder you are so dignified. What a lucky lad to have so well preserved an aunt."

To her further annoyance, Edward grinned back at him.

"She's only a half aunt really, Sir."

"Half a loaf is better than no bread. I only wish any portion of my aunts was half as attractive. Dragons the lot of them!"

Arabella bridled but bit back the angry retort. Her tormentor turned again to Edward.

"I can't pretend to be pleased about your arrival. It's deucedly inconvenient. You'll both have to come ashore with me. The ship goes further along the coast after we've landed our cargo but I daren't leave you to the Captain's tender mercies. Given half a chance he'd have you tipped overboard."

"What about my boat?" put in Edward anxiously.

"It'll be taken care of. I'll leave word with Sam where you can fetch it from. But . . ." A warning note deepened his voice. The laughter died out of his grey eyes leaving them stern, "if we help you, you must forget you ever saw him here—or any of us. I'm sure you wouldn't want to see any of us hang. Understood?"

Shaken they nodded acceptance of his condition. There was a bustle of activity on deck. At a low call from above, Tom hurried away, only pausing to tell them:

"I'll send Jack to fetch you when all's ready. Come quickly but above all silently."

As the door closed behind him, all Arabella's pent up indignation burst out.

"Insufferable creature!"

Edward protested:

"He seems a decent enough chap. You're upset because he wasn't struck all of a heap by your charms."

Arabella tossed her red gold curls.

"A great ill-mannered monster like that! I'd be insulted if he was."

"Be honest, Bella. You've been spoiled by all the flattery you get from those decrepit old dotards Father brings home."

"If you imagine I enjoy them fawning on me and pawing . . ."

Before the quarrel could develop, the bearded sailor was at the door. Hoarsely he whispered:

"Come along quick. The boat is ready. Quietly does it or we'll have every Exciseman for fifty miles on our track."

Edward leaped forward eagerly. Arabella gritted her teeth and followed. However frightened she was, she did not intend to show it. She would give that sarcastic Tom no opportunity to mock at her cowardice.

2

Up on deck the chill breeze struck at them. Arabella shivered. The clammy swirls of mist still wreathed about the ship. It was not as dense as earlier but still thick enough to hide the shore.

Sailors, their dark jackets fastened, moved busily about the ship. Heaving small wooden casks up out of the hold, they hoisted them on one shoulder and carried them to the far side of the ship where they lowered them into a small craft which lay alongside. There, more sailors stowed the kegs neatly.

Apart from automatically shielding their faces from the newcomers, they took no notice of Arabella and Edward's arrival.

"Brandy, most likely," hissed Edward, in answer to Arabella's wordless query.

She slowed her pace, wanting to see more, but there was no time to dawdle. Jack's great hand in the small of her back, propelled her firmly on to where an excited Edward was already dancing impatiently.

Bobbing in the swell beneath them, lay a small row boat. Sam sat stolidly in the center grasping the oars. Tom stood beside him. At his brusque nod Edward clambered eagerly over the rail, shinned down the ladder hanging from the ship's side, then dropped lightly into the boat. Tom motioned him past Sam then gave the signal for Arabella to join them.

She had watched with dismay Edward's progress down the swaying rope ladder, doubting whether she could negotiate that with any semblance of dignity. All the same, it would never do to be left behind. She tugged her billowing skirts firmly around her and made to step forward. Before she knew what was happening the decision had been taken for her. Jack's huge hands clamped around her waist,

17

swung her off her feet and she felt herself tossed into
Tom's waiting arms. Just as if she were a sack of meal!

She opened her mouth to protest but Tom's stern glare
cut off all but the first enraged gasp. Belatedly remembering his warning, she subsided into the empty seat. For
her own sake she would be silent, she resolved, not his.
Discovery by the Excise would prove decidedly unpleasant
for her too. Having his half sister and son dragged off to
jail by the Revenue men would undoubtedly raise Joseph's
fury to the boiling point. So however irksome it might be
to suffer this discourteous treatment silently, she would not
voice her disapproval.

As soon as she was settled, Tom sat beside Sam and
gripped the second oar. Jack cast them loose, dropping the
painter neatly beside Edward. He leaned and deftly
shoved the nose of the boat towards land, then straightened to wave a cheery hand in farewell.

Once clear of the ship's side, the two men pulled stoutly
at their oars. They moved more silently than Arabella
would have deemed possible till she noticed the dark rags
around the rollocks to muffle any sound.

Even seated, Tom's huge frame towered above Sam but
Sam's thickset body was equally powerful. The muscles
rippled on each man's arms as they sped the boat towards
the shore.

Despite the similarities in the two suntanned figures,
there was again that vast difference. Sam looked what
he was—a plain fisherman. The determined set of Tom's
head, his clear level gaze, proclaimed that here was a
man accustomed to give orders not receive them. What
was such a man doing, clad in rough seaman's garb,
mixed up with a crew of smugglers?

Looking up, Tom met her perplexed glance and raised
a quizzical eyebrow. Annoyed to have betrayed any
interest in him, she turned away and stared stonily shore-
wards.

A hazy glow shone out where someone held a lantern
to guide them in.

In a few minutes the boat ground gently on to the
pebbly shore. Sam shipped his oar and, wading through

the waves, dragged the boat more firmly on to the beach. Edward splashed through the few feet of shallow water to help him.

Arabella stood up, ready to follow them, yet reluctant to venture into the water and wet feet already unpleasantly cold from their earlier soaking.

As she hesitated, the decision was once again made for her. Tom unceremoniously lifted her off her feet and carried her ashore as easily as if she were a baby in arms. Arabella stiffened in angry protest, unaccustomed to this cavalier treatment.

"Put me down!" she commanded, furiously pummeling his chest with her fists.

His whispered reply, though low pitched, held the familiar mocking note.

"Keep still, drat you, or I'll drop you in!"

For a furious moment she glared into his dancing grey eyes, then she subsided, suspecting that he would readily carry out his threat.

The grin broadened. Rigid with fury, Arabella suffered the indignity of being carried not just ashore but right across the shingle beach. Under the shelter of the cliff Tom dumped her, none too gently, on to her feet. With an angry toss of her tangled curls, she stalked over to join Edward.

The gesture was wasted. Already Tom's attention was on other things. With a brief muttered:

"Wait here and for Heaven's sake keep quiet." Tom hurried off to where the small craft they had seen loading earlier, was busy unloading its cargo of kegs. For such a large man—surely well over six feet tall, Arabella judged —Tom was surprisingly quick and agile.

Irritated to find herself again staring at him, Arabella looked back to where they had landed. Sam had lost no time in relaunching the boat. Already he was almost swallowed up in the mist.

The beach was busy with dark figures, passing and repassing in the mist. As Tom moved among them the scene grew more orderly. A word here and there and the men began to work more purposefully.

The ragged smocks worn by many of them, revealed that these were farm laborers, trying to earn a few extra shillings to supplement their starvation wages. Men in need of a leader to coordinate their efforts—a need which Tom obviously supplied.

With renewed enthusiasm, they responded to his presence, scrunching across the shingle carrying kegs from the boat over to where a line of pack ponies patiently waited. Contentedly munching at the contents of their nosebags, the beasts made no sound but calmly accepted the burdens fastened to their broad flanks.

Edward was gazing at the scene, totally enthralled. Arabella had to dig a finger into his ribs to attract his attention.

Leaning closer, she breathed:

"Do you know where we are, Ned?"

Still intent on the busy scene he murmured:

"Don't you recognize it? We're just below the cliff where we picnicked last autumn. Where you painted that vile watercolor Mamma admired so."

Arabella chuckled softly.

"The one she said showed a proper ladylike restraint?"

Not that Sarah had really liked the painting, she reflected. The unwonted praise had been merely part of Sarah's attempt to puff her off to Sir Giles Farnham. Sarah had been hoping that he might offer for Arabella and rid Sarah of her unwanted sister-in-law. It was lucky that Sarah had never discovered why he lost interest so quickly.

As if following her thoughts, Edward chuckled.

"Do you remember? That was the day you slapped that pot-bellied old baronet and kicked his shins."

Arabella giggled, remembering Sir Giles' astonished indignation.

"Served him right. He tried to kiss me. Ugh! It was horrid. All wet and slobbery."

"No wonder he was so honest about your picture. Mamma was quite shocked."

Arabella ignored the criticism. She knew herself to be an untalented artist in spite of her enthusiasm. That day, she had tried in vain to convey the sunny calm of the scene. It was hard to believe that this grim unfriendly beach was the same spot, but she trusted Edward's judgment.

He had inherited his grandfather's gift of picking out the essentials of a landscape. With him as guide, they were rarely lost—on land or sea. Today had been an exception.

A trickle of earth fell on to her hair. Shaking it off, she peered up. A dark shape moved at the top of the cliff, dislodging a few pebbles. They slid down the cliff face, gathering other debris in a tiny avalanche.

She stared up at the cloud wreathed cliff top. Had an incautious sheep, grazing too near the edge, started the fall? As the shadowy form moved again, she picked out the shape of a three-cornered hat. This was no sheep. Her eyes growing more accustomed to the misty gloom, she gradually distinguished the shapes of two men, bent stealthily forward, intent on the activity at the water's edge.

Pressing closer against the cliff, she tugged at Edward's arm and pointed anxiously upwards.

"Excisemen?" she breathed.

For a few moments, Edward stared in the direction her quivering finger indicated.

"Looks like it. We'd best warn Tom."

In spite of the antagonism Arabella felt towards the impudent smuggler, she did not hesitate. Smuggling was a capital offense. She would not want to see even her worst enemy hang.

Cautiously they crept around to where the ponies munched peacebly. Keeping carefully out of the line of vision of the silent watchers above, they were confident that their progress went unnoticed. Even the noise of their feet, sliding on the shingle, would be lost in the crash of the waves pounding on the shore.

Once level with the pack pony line, they waited impatiently for Tom to draw near. As, at last, he approached, they moved out to intercept him.

"I told you to stay out of the way!" he hissed angrily but his anger quickly vanished as Edward explained.

"Only two men? Where?"

He seized Edward's arm.

"Don't point! We don't want them to realize they've been spotted. Just tell me exactly where you saw them."

"They're hidden in the grasses at the cliff edge, directly above the place where you ordered us to wait," Arabella butted in.

Tom ignored the resentful phrasing, asking urgently:

"You're sure they didn't realize you'd seen them? Good! Then we've a chance."

He spoke tersely to two burly smugglers. They nodded and walked casually away till they reached the foot of the cliffs. Then, as the misty shadows swallowed them up, they turned and skirted swiftly around to where a steep path wound down. Even from close to, it was hard to pick them out. The watchers on the cliff top would not have a chance of seeing them.

The last few kegs were being fastened onto the ponies. In response to a low whistle, one man moved to the head of each beast, pulled off its nosebag and grasped its halter. At a second whistle:

"Whoa, there," came the gentle call and the ponies moved forward.

Edward chuckled as Arabella's mouth fell open.

"They train the ponies to move at 'Whoa' and stop for 'Gee up.' Then, if an Exciseman calls for them to halt, they can shout 'Whoa' and gallop off. If he catches them, they pretend that the pony bolted."

Arabella had no breath to spare for a reply. The line of ponies was moving swiftly up a narrow track. Her breath came in great gasps as she forced herself to keep pace with them.

Their hooves bound up, the ponies made little sound. They scrambled over the rough ground, far more sure-footed, despite their burdens, than was Arabella.

All her energies concentrated on keeping up with the ponies, she had completely forgotten the watchers. So she was taken by surprise when they made their move.

As the last pony scrambled on to level ground, a dark figure started up from a clump of brambles:

"Halt or I fire!"

A long muzzle, pointing unwaveringly at them, reinforced the command. At Tom's nod, the leading pony driver halted his beast and the whole string wound slowly to a standstill. As they stood indecisively, a second figure stood up beside the first, pistol at the ready.

Moving cautiously toward the smugglers, the first man ordered:

"Stand clear from the ponies."

Heart thumping against her ribs, mouth dry, Arabella moved to obey his command. In that one dreadful moment a kaleidoscope of vivid pictures flashed through her terrified brain—herself languishing in jail; Joseph's furious face as he discovered that she had involved Edward in her disgrace; Sarah's self-satisfied smirk when her prophecies of the dire consequences of Arabella's wild behavior were proved justified.

Then, with a surge of hope, she caught sight of two shadowy figures, creeping stealthily up behind the Excisemen. She gave a gasp of horror as each raised a heavy cudgel, winced involuntarily as the blows fell. With a low moan, one Exciseman pitched forward, and lay still.

His fellow, catching some sound at the last second, leaped aside. The cudgel missed his head, crashing down on his shoulder. The blow made him stagger but he recovered quickly and fired blindly.

The ball whistled harmlessly past the smuggler but the report echoed loudly over the silent cliff top. Another moment and the smuggler had overpowered his victim and wrested away the pistol but the damage was done.

Behind her, Arabella heard Tom curse softly.

"We must hurry. That shot will bring up their companions. Tie up the pair of them and leave them in the brambles there."

Under the dark stain that concealed their features, Arabella could distinguish the alarm in the smugglers' faces. This incident had upset them too.

At first the Excisemen lay so still that she feared the savage blows had killed them but, as the smugglers tied them up, their feeble struggles reassured her. She felt it callous and wrong to leave them thus but knew that the smugglers would never permit her to aid their captives. All she could do was pray that the other revenue officers would soon arrive to free them.

The line of ponies moved off once more. She was hurried along with them. Stumbling over the uneven tussocks, every muscle aching, she found it impossible to match their pace. She lurched forward as her foot caught in a clump of thistles. A firm hand steadied her. Tom's voice sounded low in her ear.

"Not far now. There are horses in the lane."

Wearily she plodded on. A few minutes later, she caught the soft snuffle of two horses. A man stood between them, whispering to calm them.

The line of ponies passed through the gateway and walked steadily up the lane. At the crossroads they split up.

Before long they were all out of sight. Even the dull sound of their muffled hooves had died away. Tom turned, with relief, to Arabella and Edward.

"Right! They know what they must do. Now all that remains is to get you two safely away."

Arabella looked with misgivings at the spirited horses. Only two of them and no side saddle. How would they cope?

Tom grinned at her dismayed expression.

"You'll both have to ride pillion. It won't be far and fortunately you're both light weights."

He swung up into the saddle of the massive grey and motioned his companion to lift Arabella in front. The wiry man mounted the bay and Edward scrambled up behind him.

The sound of horses galloping came clearly through the mist. Tom exclaimed grimly.

"This will be the others attracted by that cursed shot. We'll have to draw them off to give the ponies a chance to get the cargo clear."

Before any of them realized what he intended, he had leaned forward, pulled a pistol from the saddle holster and fired it. As her ears stopped ringing, Arabella was

aware of a confused shouting in the distance and the
pounding of galloping hooves sounded ever nearer.

"Hold tight," warned Tom. He wheeled his horse
around. The bay followed obediently back through the
gateway. As they retraced their route across the cliff top,
the sound of their pursuers grew steadily louder. Arabella
peered back in alarm as a shot whistled over her head.
The four horsemen, pounding behind, were clearly gaining
on them.

"Faster! They'll catch us. Faster!" she gasped but Tom
took no notice. He kept the grey down to a steady canter.
Arabella looked anxiously around. Where were they head-
ing and why?

As they drew closer to the cliff edge, she suddenly
clutched fearfully at Tom. Straight into their path rolled
a bound figure, kicking and struggling. One of the Excisemen had recovered sufficiently to move from the
bramble patch. Hearing them approach, he had plainly
imagined them to be his friends, come to rescue him.

The bay swung wide to avoid him but Tom made no
attempt to turn his horse. Arabella screamed in horror,
as they rode straight at the writhing figure, terrified lest
they trample him. Then, at the last moment, she felt Tom
tug at the rein and the grey swerved aside.

Tom steadied his mount momentarily, then his feet dug
into the horse's side and they leaped forward, in a full
gallop at last. Alongside them, the bay thundered neck
to neck. Arabella had a brief glimpse of Erward's face,
alight with rapture. It seemed that he, at least, was enjoying this wild chase.

Forgetful of her dignity, she clung tightly to Tom's
jacket, her face pressed into his chest.

"Stop in the name of the Law!" came a faint call behind them and another shot screamed past and another.

Then the shouting died away and she could hear nothing but the wind whistling by and the drum of their
horses' hooves. Amazingly, she felt no fear now. Pressed
so close against Tom that she could feel his heart beating,
she felt perfectly secure. The strong arm that encircled
her would guard her from any harm. Indeed, her strongest

sensation was one of exhilaration. Fancifully, she imagined that this must be how the ladies of the ballads
felt, as they galloped off across the saddle bows of their
lovers.

She flushed, suddenly embarrassed at the idea, and
pulled herself a little away from Tom. His arm tightened
around her drawing her close again.

Gradually the horses' mad speed slackened.

"They've stopped to free their friends," Tom declared
in satisfied tones.

Seeing Edward's amused glance, Arabella struggled into
a more decorous position. They wound their way through
a maze of lanes. Further inland the mist was clearing and
Arabella was astonished to realize that it was still daylight.
So much had happened in the past hour that it seemed
strange that so little time had, in fact, elapsed.

After all the excitement, it was pleasant to ride gently
between flower-decked hedgerows. By branching off on
footpaths here and there, they skirted around the villages,
scarcely meeting anyone on their way.

Eventually they came to paths that Arabella recognized.
Now she was even more anxious that they should not be
seen. She could picture Joseph's horrified reaction to
gossip about his half-sister, seen sharing a horse with a
stranger.

It was with a mixture of relief and regret that she saw,
in front of them, the imposing gates of Ridware Hall—
Joseph's latest attempt to proclaim his prosperity to their
neighborhood.

Tom dismounted and lifted her gently to the ground,
then stood smiling disturbingly down at her. Suddenly shy,
she could not meet his gaze. Eyes downcast, she murmured disjointed thanks. He brushed them aside.

"It is I who must thank you—both of you. But for
your warning, we might all have been in prison now."

He reached out to shake Edward's hand. Then, before
she realized what he was doing, he had raised Arabella's
hand to his lips. She looked up wonderingly. For a long
moment grey eyes gazed deep into green. The expression

in Tom's eyes was unfathomable. Then the wicked twinkle reappeared and he chuckled softly.

"I said he was a lucky lad. Any of my aunts would have had hysterics!"

He remounted swiftly, and rode away.

Arabella stared after him, the hand he had kissed pressed to her cheek. That had been a strange gesture for such a man. Odd too, that the Sussex accent had vanished totally from Tom's speech. Who was Tom?

Edward's impatient voice broke through her perplexed thoughts.

"Come on, Bella. We must hurry. Father will be furious if we're late."

Joseph! The thought of his pompous disapproval brought her back to reality. Fancies forgotten, she hastened after Edward.

3

The ornate gilt clock on the mantel was striking six as they crept into the hall. Joseph insisted on rigorous punctuality. Dinner was served precisely at six. They looked round apprehensively but only Hamstall was in sight. The butler stared impassively back at the bedraggled couple.

Moving swiftly between Hamstall and the drawing room, Edward smiled coaxingly.

"Can't you hold dinner up, for a few minutes, Hamstall?" he urged. "Just enough to let us tidy up."

Pursing his lips disapprovingly, Hamstall shook his head.

"Mr. Edward! What a suggestion. Do you want me to lose my position?"

Edward turned away disconsolately.

"No. I suppose it's better that we should get into trouble than you. We can't go into dinner like this. We'll have to be late and brave it out."

"Would you please tell my brother that we will be down shortly if he should inquire after us," Arabella was ruefully aware that the dignified request suited oddly with her unkempt appearance.

The stout figure coughed gently.

"You have presumably not yet heard, Miss Arabella. Dinner will be at seven this evening. Mr. Ridware sent word that he had been detained."

Edward turned back with a chuckle of reluctant admiration.

"Hamstall, you old fraud! I might have known you were roasting us."

Arabella too smiled at the butler.

"That is certainly a stroke of luck for us, Hamstall,

but I'll warrant the message caused some confusion in the kitchen."

A faint smile flitted across the normally impassive face.

"The foreign person was somewhat eloquent on the subject, Miss. These French individuals have not our habits of self-control. He is, however, now attempting to cope."

Arabella smiled back, well aware of the bitter feud between the butler and Joseph's new chef, who had supplanted Hamstall's sister. Desire to be in the fashion had, for once, overcome Joseph's natural suspicion of foreigners. He had engaged Monsieur Dubois as chef, listening sympathetically to his story of the loyalty that caused him to follow his émigré master into exile. Arabella had questioned why that loyalty had permitted him to abandon the Comte so readily once in England, but Joseph, his belly full of Monsieur Dubois' excellently cooked dinners, refused to listen to such quibbles. His sister had to allow that her dislike of the man's appearance—his hangdog expression and the shifty eyes—had biased her against him.

Although she sympathized with Hamstall she knew it unwise openly to take sides.

"Well, at all events, the delay has proved a blessing for us. Come along Edward. You look as if you'd been dragged through a hedge backwards."

Edward drew an indignant breath.

"I look as if . . . You should see yourself! She looks a proper hoyden, doesn't she Hamstall?"

Again Hamstall coughed gently.

"If I might be permitted to suggest, Miss Arabella, you might be wise to go straight to your room. Mrs. Ridware and Mrs. Joseph are already in the drawing room."

Arabella did not require a second hint. The sound of voices might arouse Sarah's curiosity and for Sarah, or mother, to see her in this state would be disastrous.

Upstairs, Mollie was waiting to help her dress for dinner. As the door opened she exclaimed reproachfully:

"Thank goodness you're back, Miss Bella. I was be-

ginning . . ." she broke off with a shriek of horror as she
took in Arabella's disheveled appearance.

"My gracious, what a pickle! What would your mamma
say?"

Arabella bore the scolding philosophically. Mollie
might chide but she would never betray her to mamma
or Joseph. Originally Arabella's nurse, Mollie was still
inclined to treat her mistress as a naughty child, but she
was fiercely loyal. Once she had rebuked Arabella it was
over and done with and Mollie would defend her staunchly from anyone else's censure.

Still grumbling, Mollie poured water into the china
bowl for Arabella to wash. She helped her pull off the
bedraggled day dress and fetched a muslin evening gown.
She stooped disapprovingly to pick up the stockings that
Arabella had peeled off.

"Just look at the state these are in. Soaked through.
Ruined they are and likely you've caught your death of
cold, flitting around with your feet all wet. Whatever have
you been up to, Miss Bella, to get into such a dreadful
mess?"

Arabella, busy pulling on clean white silk tights, paused,
smiling mischievously.

"I've been sailing with Edward, Mollie, but don't tell
anyone."

"Off in that boat. Miss Arabella you must be out of
your mind! With all those rascally Frenchies waiting to
come and murder us all. It's a wonder Boney didn't
catch you."

Dimples peeped out of Arabella's cheeks as she smiled
reminiscently:

"We thought he had once for a moment!"

She gave Mollie a carefully edited version of their
adventures. Mollie was horrified.

"Let's hope Mr. Joseph doesn't get to hear of these
goings on. Nor your poor mamma. The worry of it would
kill her."

Arabella's dimples appeared again, briefly.

"I promise not to tell them if you don't."

Mollie merely grunted her disapproval of this impudent suggestion, and began to brush the tangles vigorously from her mistress' red gold curls.

"I suppose it could be worse. You could have met up with some rascally young good for nothing . . ." she broke off abruptly as Arabella gave a guilty start, demanding:

"What's the matter now, Miss Bella? Surely you haven't gone and fallen in love with one of those nasty smugglers?"

"Of course not! You pulled my hair. That's all," Arabella retorted indignantly but Mollie's words had come a little too close to the truth. Not, of course, she told herself severely, that she had fallen in love with anyone. It was just hard to forget Tom. The excitement of that wild ride still tingled within her and the memory of the long moment when their eyes had met. Tom had broken the spell with a flippant comment but she found it harder to recover from.

She stared at her reflection in the full length mirror. Her cheeks glowed, green eyes sparkled. Then she caught sight of the troubled expression on Mollie's face, reflected behind hers, and smiled reassuringly. Mollie eyed her dubiously.

"I don't know what mischief you're up to, Miss Bella, nor I don't want to know. But I warn you—Mr. Joseph won't stand for it. Not like the poor master used to."

Arabella hugged her briefly.

"Don't worry, Mollie. I'll be sensible."

She stood meekly while Mollie pulled the clean gown carefully over her head, tied the brilliant green sash and threaded matching green ribbon to loop up the fiery curls.

It was five minutes to seven when she entered the drawing room. Everyone was waiting save Joseph. Edward, spruce now in his new blue jacket and white breeches, dark hair neatly brushed, gave her a conspiratorial wink.

"There you are at last, Arabella," Sarah's voice had that querulous note it habitually bore. "We were wondering what had become of you."

Arabella smiled, determined not to be tempted into any rash rejoinder.

"Hamstall told me that dinner would be late so I didn't hurry down."

"Indeed! No one troubled to inform me till I was already downstairs. Charlotte and I have been waiting here an age."

Arabella smiled even more sweetly:

"I am sure that my brother had a good reason to keep us all waiting."

Personally she considered it a deplorable habit of Joseph's to keep everyone else hungry if he was delayed. Especially annoying in one who demanded such precise punctuality in others. Father had always expected them to begin dinner without him if he were late and either slipped in to join them in the second course or had a tray in his room but such casual habits did not suit with Joseph's dignity.

Sarah's hasty denial of any criticism of her dear spouse was probably as insincere as Arabella's defense of him. Beside Sarah, sixteen year old Charlotte, whose plump figure looked even worse than usual in a tight pink muslin gown, fidgeted unhappily.

"I wish Papa would hurry. Why does he keep us waiting? I'm famished."

Sarah's plaintive voice immediately sharpened in rebuke. Charlotte apologized sulkily.

Arabella took a seat beside her own mother. Slim and frail in her widow's weeds, she looked years younger than Sarah, though they were actually separated in age by only a few months.

Discontent had scored Sarah's face and strands of grey showed in her lank hair, where Arabella's mother still cherished her unlined pink and white complexion and any white hairs were lost among the gold. Equally unfairly, the unrelieved black of her mourning clothes suited her to perfection. Sarah's lavender silk, far more expensive and elaborately fashionable, merely accentuated her sallow complexion and general shapelessness.

It must be very galling for Sarah to be so outshone by

her mother-in-law, thought Arabella with a sudden rush of sympathy. Indeed, the day `father had arrived home with the young heiress as his second bride, must have proved a profound shock for both Sarah and Joseph.

To do them justice, they had obviously welcomed the young bride kindly enough. She had been too shy and inexperienced to want to take over the running of the household and Sarah had willingly continued to hold the reins—with just sufficient grumbling to insure that no one forgot how onerous a task it was.

The Captain's death had made little difference to their everyday lives. Only now, as his heir, Joseph administered what he had, for years, managed for his father and Sarah had the satisfaction of knowing herself mistress by right as well as custom.

With Arabella's mother continuing to provide a large proportion of the money required to run the hall, they were pleased to have her stay with them. Even Arabella, chafing at the irritations of life with Joseph, acknowledged that her mother would be incapable of successfully setting up her own household.

As seven struck Joseph bustled in.

"You'll have to forgive my coming in in all my dirt, my dear, but I am later than I expected. I'm too hungry to go to all the bother of changing so I've informed Hamstall that he can serve dinner immediately."

No word of apology for keeping them all waiting, thought Arabella indignantly. She surveyed her brother's stout form critically. Not yet forty, Joseph already had a heavy paunch. Despite the entreaties of his fashion-conscious wife, he continued to wear a small tie wig. Arabella strongly suspected that this was to hide the sad thinning of his own hair. Since the iniquitous tax on powder he had abandoned the pounce box and let the wig remain its natural indifferent brown. As she walked behind him into the dining room she caught the faint creak that betrayed that Joseph had copied the Prince of Wales' fashion of wearing a corset to control his surplus flesh.

The dinner was not too badly ruined. The lamb was somewhat black at the edges but the fish seemed, if anything, improved by the extra cooking, and the tarts and pastries were as delicious as ever.

Having conformed to fashion and engaged a French chef, Joseph characteristically insisted that the poor man provide good English food. Only when visitors came was Monsieur Dubois permitted to display his true culinary skills. Arabella often wondered why he consented to remain in Joseph's service. It was not even as if Joseph was a generous master. Willing to spend money like water to make a great effect, he was remarkably tightfisted over the smaller details.

His first hunger assuaged by a huge plateful of lamb followed by rabbit pie and washed down by a tankard of ale, Joseph was eager to tell them all his news.

"Smuggling in broad daylight this afternoon. I don't know what things are coming to."

"You could hardly call this afternoon's fog broad daylight," objected Edward. He relapsed into silence as his father ordered him roundly to hold his tongue.

Joseph continued:

"The revenue officers had been warned to expect a landing . . ."

Edward burst out:

"You mean that some wretch had betrayed the smugglers?"

Joseph glared angrily at the fresh interruption.

"I meant what I said. Some person with a proper feeling of what he owes to his country informed the revenue officers that those scoundrelly smugglers intended to land a cargo today. Exactly where he could not tell them so a couple of officers were sent to every likely place."

"Did they catch the smugglers, Papa?" asked Charlotte eagerly.

Joseph looked a little more pleased at his daughter's enthusiastic reaction.

"Unfortunately no. Two of the officers did surprise a band of the wretches and attempted to apprehend them but they were brutally assaulted and left for dead. Their colleagues were attracted by the noise of their desperate struggle and bravely pursued the smugglers for some considerable distance before losing them in the thick mist."

"How thrilling!" Charlotte breathed a fat sigh, "I wish I could have seen them."

With a shudder Arabella tried to imagine Charlotte's reaction if she had been there. Even the sight of a mouse in her room sent her into hysterics.

Charlotte turned impulsively to Edward.

"Didn't you see anything of this affair, Edward?"

Her brother glared balefully at her.

"I didn't see anything at all like that while I was out *riding* this afternoon."

Arabella bit back a giggle—what he said was true enough. It had not been in the least like the scene Joseph described.

Charlotte ignored her brother's warning tone.

"Riding? I thought you said . . ."

Edward butted ruthlessly in:

"Pass me the grapes, Charlotte," he hissed.

As there were none on the table and he and Arabella had caught Charlotte only that morning greedily devouring the last bunch in the hot house, Charlotte colored and fell silent, correctly interpreting the threat. If she betrayed that Edward had been sailing then he would tell of her misdemeanor—and grapes were Joseph's favorite fruit too.

Arabella hastened to fill the awkward gap in the conversation before Joseph could demand what all the whispering was about.

"But were none of the smugglers captured, Joseph?"

The pompous red face turned in her direction.

"Alas no! I regret to say that not one of the traitors was taken."

"Traitors!" burst out Edward indignantly, "Why call them traitors for just running a few kegs of brandy ashore?"

Joseph's face darkened ominously.

"What else can one call them when they supply gold and information to that infidel Bonaparte?"

"Nonsense, Father, they are just poor laborers trying

to earn a few extra coppers to keep their children from starving."

The veins bulged alarmingly across Joseph's now purple forehead as he spluttered:

"Poor fellows indeed! Will you call them poor fellows when Bonaparte lands and they rise up to murder us like their fellow cutthroats did across the channel?"

"It isn't at all the same. Those French peasants were terribly oppressed. We must be careful not to make the same errors here."

Even Edward himself realized he had gone too far this time. Joseph gobbled at his son like a great red turkey-cock, then he slammed his fist down on the table, roaring:

"I'll have none of that damned Jacobin talk in my house!"

Arabella smiled sweetly at him.

"But Joseph, I thought that even Mr. Fox once sympathized with the French people?"

Joseph glared at her.

"Maybe he did but he admits his error now. Even the wisest of us may change his opinions."

She hid a smile at this pompous declaration. Joseph's own politics had undergone a radical alteration. Once the truest of blue Tories, he had objected so violently to Mr. Pitt's revolutionary new tax on income that he had immediately become the most obstinate of Whigs.

Sometimes she suspected that the presence of the Prince of Wales and his Whig friends in nearby Brighton helped to keep Joseph in that party. Though undoubtedly a gentleman, Joseph was not entirely acceptable to the top lofty Tory aristocracy of the neighborhood. She wondered whether he hoped to push himself more easily into the less rigid Whig social scene.

Sarah had seen the tell-tale twitching at her husband's temple and hastened to change the subject.

"Did you visit Sir George, my love?"

Joseph's face brightened.

"Yes indeed, my dear. He agrees that we must organize some sort of volunteer corps. We were discussing the matter when the news came about those rascally smugglers. From the confusion, we imagined at first that the French had landed."

"An understandable error," murmured Edward with a brief grin at Arabella.

His father scowled at them.

"We went to question the smugglers' victims to find out whether they could furnish us with any description of their assailants but they could give us little information. The miscreants were too heavily disguised to be recognizable. Some of the cowardly wretches even wore women's clothes."

Edward nearly choked in his efforts to conceal his involuntary whoop of mirth. His father glared.

"Such are the scoundrels you uphold, Edward. Cutthroats, vagabonds, the scum of the earth, ready to flock to Bonaparte's rascally French forces once they land."

"*If* they land," Arabella's voice cut coolly through the peroration.

"No need to be complacent about it, Miss. Heaven help you when they do come! No woman—young or old —will be safe from the villains."

They finished the meal in silence. Arabella was heartily glad when Sarah rose to lead the ladies out.

"Arabella, my love, I wish you would not quarrel so with your brother," her mother's gentle voice was reproachful.

"But Mamma, he makes such ridiculous statements."

"Nevertheless you should have more respect for him, Arabella. Dear Joseph was so kind to us both when your poor dear Papa . . ." the widow's voice trailed away as the ready tears filled her eyes.

Her daughter watched awkwardly, embarrassed as always by the open display of emotion. Mrs. Ridware gave a watery smile.

"Try for my sake, dearest.. It makes me so uncomfortable to hear you squabble."

"I'll try," Arabella had the uneasy feeling that she had made and broken this promise too many times already.

Sarah's plaintive tones interrupted them:

"Fanny, my silks are all in a tangle. Will you unravel them?"

Arabella resented this treatment of her mother as some sort of poor relation—a drudge for Sarah. It was even more infuriating that her mother should seem perfectly content in the role. She moved obediently to the stool beside Sarah's couch and began gently to tease the threads apart.

Impatiently Arabella went over to the piano. There was a new piece of music on the stand, left from Charlotte's lesson that morning. Arabella had thought it an attractive tune, even when massacred by Charlotte and was eager to try it herself. She picked out the notes, slowly at first then more confidently, humming the words softly to herself.

"Very nice, my dear!"

She had been so engrossed in her playing that she had not heard Joseph enter the room. As he leaned over her, patting her shoulder approvingly, the brandy fumes were strong on his breath. Obviously Joseph had drunk himself into a better humor. He smiled expansively at her.

"Very nice indeed. Practice hard, Arabella. We have a special visitor coming soon. I want you to make a good impression on him."

Arabella's heart sank at the arch significance in his voice. She had lost count of the number of "special visitors" that Joseph had brought home on her behalf. He must be desperate to be rid of her. Sarah had pricked up her ears.

"Visitor, Joseph? Who is he pray? We are anxious to hear all about him, are we not, Arabella?"

Her sister-in-law ignored her. Undaunted Joseph plowed on:

"He is a Captain Henri Desormais."

"A Frenchman?"

Sarah's surprise was understandable. Her husband's opinion of the French was not generally high.

"An émigré. He was brought up in this country. I met him in London last month. He is a member of the Prince of Wales' household and hopes to come to Brighton shortly when His Royal Highness moves to Pavilion for the summer."

"Indeed!" Sarah's pursed lips showed her thoughts on the Prince of Wales and his raffish set.

Joseph hastened to reassure her.

"No, my dear. He is a very respectable gentleman. Not at all wild."

"I am glad to hear it."

Arabella was less satisfied by the assurance. She had a sneaking suspicion that she might prefer a man that Joseph would consider wild. His previous choices had been anything but attractive. Obviously Edward agreed.

"I hope this Captain is more presentable than the baronet who was dangling after Bella last year."

"I missed him but he couldn't be worse than that doddery old Mr. Morpeth," giggled Charlotte.

"That is quite enough, children," warned Sarah coldly. "It is not polite to mock two such estimable gentlemen. Arabella would have been very fortunate if either of them had condescended to offer for her."

"Condescended!" Edward whistled in amazement. "I'd have thought they'd have been only too happy to get their hands on her £10,000."

"There is no necessity to be vulgar, Edward," snapped his mother. "Neither of the gentlemen was in the slightest degree impoverished."

"Certainly not," echoed Joseph. "We're not encouraging any fortune hunters to dangle after Arabella."

That was true enough, thought Arabella despondently. Joseph was quick to chase away an amusing young officer or dandy though she felt she would rather marry one of them than the elderly suitors her brother had produced. After all, she had money enough to support them but Joseph rarely looked at things her way.

Sarah, she knew, would be less fussy. Sarah was desperately anxious to marry Arabella off before Charlotte was launched into society. It would be false modesty to deny that, as Edward had phrased it—bluntly but incontrovertibly:

"No one is going to look at Charlotte when Arabella is in the room."

When Arabella had not only the looks but the fortune, Charlotte was cast very much in the shade. No doubt Sarah would hold the ladder gladly for Arabella, should she wish to elope—though Sarah would naturally prefer "a good marriage." Then Arabella would be able to sponsor Charlotte into society and later her younger sisters, one at school, two still in the nursery.

"But, Papa!" Charlotte was still bursting with curiosity. "You haven't told us anything about Captain Desormais yet. Is he young and handsome?"

Joseph beamed benevolently.

"I suppose you ladies might think so, my dear. Not that I consider such trifles important, but the Captain seems a fine figure of a man."

Charlotte pressed pudgy hands together ecstatically:

"Oh Papa. How exciting. Aren't you dying with impatience to see this young man, Bella?"

"Not really," replied Arabella coolly. "I know by now that I can rely on your Papa's taste."

Edward grinned appreciatively but Joseph was oblivious of her irony.

"You will not have to contain your impatience for long, my dears. I saw Captain Desormais briefly today. He was on only a flying visit but promises to dine with us when he returns next week. Then you can form your own opinions."

He brushed away the rest of Charlotte's eager queries and snored the rest of the evening away in his armchair.

After all the excitements of the day, Arabella was glad to retire early but although she soon fell asleep it was a troubled sleep, disturbed by confused dreams. She seemed to be galloping madly across an endless cliff top pursued by Joseph mounted on a piano and shouting:

"Stop! I want you to meet Bonaparte." At least, she told herself, on waking, Captain Desormais could not be that bad—could he?

4

In the event, it was a great deal longer than a week before Arabella met Captain Desormais. First, the Prince of Wales' arrival in Brighton was delayed by official apprehension of the danger to him of being in the path of the expected invasion. Then when braving the dangers, the prince settled with his entourage in the Pavilion, Captain Desormais found it impossible to leave his royal master for sufficient time to avail himself of Joseph's long standing invitation.

As each new engagement was broken, Charlotte was loud in her disappointment. Eventually, constant put-offs weakened even her enthusiasm and to everyone's relief she gave up her eager speculations about their dilatory guest.

Just as impatiently as his sister awaited the tardy Captain's arrival, Edward fretted for news of his boat. He hurried down each day to Sam's cottage but he, too, received only disappointment.

Then one evening he rushed home, face beaming with delight.

"Good news at last, Bella. Tom says that my boat will be ready tomorrow without fail."

"Tom?" she echoed in surprise.

"Yes, he's lodging with Sam now. Didn't you know?"

"You never mentioned it."

"Perhaps I didn't think you'd be interested," Edward gave her a mischievous grin, eyeing her sudden flush speculatively.

"I'm not," she snapped crossly.

Curtly she refused his invitation to come out and try the boat next morning.

"Please yourself," Edward was unconcerned, "Sam will always go with me—or Tom."

After a hasty breakfast Edward hurried out next day. Delight at the return of his boat tempted him to spend longer away than he had intended and he was disastrously late for dinner. Joseph was greatly annoyed by his unpunctuality and when an incautious word from Charlotte betrayed what had delayed Edward, his fury knew no bounds. Face swollen purple with rage, he could hardly force out the angry words.

"Are you insane? Risking your neck at sea with that fiend Bonaparte expected to invade us at any moment."

Edward darted a malevolent scowl at Charlotte.

"It was perfectly safe, Father. I saw only fishing boats all day."

"Then you were luckier than you deserve. Suppose you had been taken by the French—they would not hesitate to torture you to extract information about our defenses."

"I hardly feel that anything Edward knows would be of outstanding value to the enemy," observed Arabella coolly, in a heroic attempt to draw Joseph's fire. Bloodshot eyes swiveled in her direction and her half-brother roared:

"When I want your opinion, Miss, I'll ask for it! I've no doubt but that you've encouraged the young fool. Neither of you has the faintest scrap of common sense! That boat is not to be used! Do I make myself clear?"

Edward nodded sulkily. His father thundered on:

"Tomorrow you will make arrangements for the boat to be brought ashore. You will not hazard your safety in it again."

Edward flushed scarlet with indignation.

"I've said I won't use it. Isn't my word good enough?" Joseph glared back belligerently.

"No arguments! Do as I say. And don't be late home. Captain Desormais is to dine with us tomorrow. I don't wish him to discover what an unmannerly cub of a son I have."

His hearers paid little heed. Even Charlotte found it hard to summon up much enthusiasm as she cried:

"Oh Papa! Will he really come this time?"

Scowling at her, Joseph exclaimed testily:

"Naturally he will come, child. Why not? He told me how very upset he has felt at having to disappoint us so often."

None of his family shared Joseph's confidence in the Captain's promise, so they were agreeably surprised when, next evening, Joseph ushered an elegant stranger into the drawing room. Despite an instinctive prejudice against any suitor chosen by her half-brother, Arabella could not help but be favorably impressed.

Their guest appeared to be in his early thirties. He was slightly above medium height, his figure well formed. From the top of his glossy brown hair, worn in the fashionable Brutus cut, to the gleaming tips of his stylish Hessians, he was impeccable. Nothing in his appearance was so ultrafashionable as to seem overdone but the overall impression was of modish elegance.

Arabella stole a dissatisfied glance at her own attire, wishing belatedly that she had put on her newest outfit. Not, she reflected bitterly, that even her sprigged muslin would appear anything but countryfied to the fashionable Captain. Even the top Brighton designers lagged a little behind the London fashions, while the elderly seamstress in the village who sewed their gowns for Charlotte and Arabella, was positively antediluvian.

Pompously Joseph presented his companion to Sarah. The gallant newcomer bent gracefully over her languidly proffered hand.

"Mincing French fop!" muttered Edward disapprovingly in Arabella's ear.

Sarah smiled benignly on her guest and beside her Charlotte heaved a plumply estatic sigh. Captain Desormais bent his smile upon her.

"And this, Madame, must be your so delightful sister-in-law."

Delicately he raised Charlotte's hand to his lips. She blushed crimson with gratification and gazed adoringly into his face, too overcome to correct his error. Joseph hastened to set him right.

"No, no, my dear Sir. Charlotte here is my eldest daughter."

With an expansive gesture of amazement, the Captain turned his expressive gaze back upon Sarah.

"Your daughter, Madame? Impossible! But yes, I see now that she has her Mamma's beautiful profile."

Sarah and Charlotte beamed fatuously after him as Joseph led Captain Desormais across to where Arabella stood beside her mother.

"Fanny, may I present Captain Desormais. Captain, my Mamma-in-law, Mrs. Ridware. And this is my little sister, Arabella."

Arabella stiffened at the jocular "little." Captain Desormais bowed deeply.

"Enchanté, Madame. Mademoiselle, at last I have the honor of making your acquaintance."

As he bent to kiss her hand, Arabella thought fleetingly of the last man to salute her thus. What an immense contrast between the Captain's respectful manner and Tom's arrogance.

She found it impossible not to respond to the warm note in the Frenchman's voice and the admiration in his sparkling dark eyes. The brief doubt whether all this was not too polished to be entirely sincere, was quickly dismissed.

As Captain Desormais gallantly proffered his arm to escort her into dinner, she reveled in the novel sensation of being treated as a fragile creature. She smiled approvingly into adoring eyes that revealed not a trace of mockery. Here was a true gentleman, one who understood how a lady should be treated.

With a fellow countryman to impress, Monsieur Dubois excelled himself. Joseph contentedly gorged his way through the elaborate French dishes, though he saved face by growling:

"These fancy foreign messes are all very well now and then but give me good plain English food for choice."

Captain Desormais throughout dinner kept up an amusing flow of gossip and anecdote. He had them all smiling at his droll tales of life in Carlton House.

"Is His Royal Highness determined to settle here for the season?" inquired Joseph anxiously.

"I believe so. He naturally wishes to be near his regiment in case the enemy should decide to make this part of the coast his target."

"He is Colonel of the 10th Dragoons isn't he?" put in Edward. "Won't they give him a more responsible position now the country is so threatened?"

The Captain shook his head regretfully.

"Alas, no! His Royal Highness was anxious to play a more prominent part in his country's struggle but His Majesty the King refused to grant his request and His Royal Highness must be content with his present minor role."

"How odd."

"I believe," declared the Captain stiffly, "that His Majesty is unwilling to place the Prince in a position of any real peril as he considers it vital that the succession should not be imperiled."

"But surely, there are other princes and Princess Charlotte," Arabella objected.

"Yes, indeed, Mademoiselle, but in the present peculiar circumstances—with His Majesty's health so precarious —it is more imperative that his eldest son should be safeguarded. Should the Prince of Wales be killed or, worse still, be captured by the enemy, it might lead to a very dangerous situation."

"Personally, I'd consider that for him to be killed would be infinitely worse than merely being captured," declared Edward crushingly.

Captain Desormais shot him a look of pure dislike.

"Naturally no one, least of all myself, would wish any harm to befall His Royal Highness. I merely wished to imply that, for the country, his capture might prove even more dangerous than his death. With His Royal Highness as a hostage, Bonaparte would be in a very effective bargaining position. Especially as the shock would almost certainly affect the King's health."

They were all silent, recalling those anxious weeks when the King was last ill. Then, there were grave fears that he might never regain his sanity. Everything was in train for the Prince of Wales to be declared Regent when, happily, the King made a full recovery. It was easy to imagine the confusion should the King again be taken ill when the Prince was not available to assume the burden of royal duties.

Sarah broke the silence with an eager inquiry about the latest London modes. Her son stared, in horror.

"Mamma! You cannot expect a gentleman to interest himself in such paltry concerns."

His disgusted objection was ignored. Captain Desormais proved only too happy to enlighten the ladies as to the latest styles in the Metropolis. The ladies listened avidly. Momentarily, Arabella felt a twinge of doubt as she speculated how the Captain had gained his very comprehensive knowledge of feminine fashions but she, too, found his descriptions too enthralling to waste much time worrying about their source.

After a fascinating dissertation on the newest bonnets, Captain Desormais glanced approvingly around the table, declaring:

"Little though I find to recommend in the present régime in my native land, I must applaud the delightfully natural style of dress they have introduced. Although I am glad to see that you English ladies have adapted it to a far more elegant mode. I felt that the fashions I saw among the females in Paris were a trifle too extreme to be in perfect taste."

"You have been to France, recently?" Joseph expressed the general surprise.

"Indeed yes. His Royal Highness graciously permitted me to pay a brief visit to Paris during the peace to sort out a few affairs for my late father. Alas I found everything sadly altered. It was perhaps a blessing that my father was unable to return himself though such had been his dearest wish."

"You had no desire to remain in France yourself?"

"No, Mademoiselle. I think of England as my home. I was so young when we came—a mere boy. My roots are firmly set in England where I have so many friends." His voice deepened, "among whom I hope I may include you, Mademoiselle."

Blushing, Arabella nodded shy assent. Tonight she was disappointed to see Sarah's signal for the ladies to retire and leave the gentlemen to their wine.

In the drawing room Charlotte was loud in her praise of their guest.

"How I envy you, Bella. Such an elegant beau. I'm sure you must be in love with him already."

"My dear Charlotte, you are too boisterous." Sarah's voice was acidly disapproving. "Nothing is yet settled."

"No, Mamma, but one can see how much Captain Desormais admires Arabella. I'm sure he must wish to marry her."

"I trust Arabella is too sensible to allow her head to be turned by a little flattering attention. When the Captain declares himself, *if* he does, will be quite soon enough to be thinking of marriage. As for all this vulgar nonsense about falling in love, such ideas are most ill-bred."

Charlotte clasped pudgy red hands together, sighing:

"Oh, Mamma, how unromantic you are."

Fortunately Sarah's opinions on romance were cut short by the arrival of the tea and, soon after, the gentlemen rejoined them.

"Couldn't keep Captain Desormais away from you ladies a minute longer," boomed Joseph jocularly. "One of you must have made a conquest already. Don't you think so, Bella?"

Arabella ignored the remark and jovial nudge that accompanied it but in spite of a faintly lingering suspicion that the Captain's flattering attentions could be occasioned as much by her £10,000 as by her personal charms—she had noticed how effusive he had been to Charlotte when he arrived and how swiftly he had dropped her when he learned Arabella was the heiress—even so the Frenchman had made a favorable impression on her. It was certainly pleasant to have so considerate a companion. Yet his attentions were not vulgarly obtrusive. He listened engrossed while she played, turned the pages of her music and even, sometimes, joined unself-consciously in her song.

Warmly he begged for another song and another till she laughingly protested that he would wear her voice away.

As he escorted her back to her chair, again the thought pressed of how different was his manner from the presumptuous way in which Tom had handled her. She scowled at the memory.

Captain Desormais bent anxiously over her.

"You frown, Mademoiselle. You think me then too bold?"

She shook her head, smiling ruefully.

"I beg your pardon, Captain Desormais. I was thinking of something else. What were you saying?"

"Your sister informs me that you are fond of riding. I was bold enough to request leave to accompany you."

"I should be delighted to have your escort, Sir."

"Tomorrow?"

Arabella glanced at Sarah who nodded enthusiastically.

"I am sure dear Arabella will be most gratified if you would join her and Edward on their ride tomorrow."

Edward was far from pleased at the arrangement. He listened glowering, next morning, to all his mother's last minute instructions. Still scowling he sat astride his fidgety bay waiting with Arabella for the Captain's coming. Left to herself, Arabella would have remained indoors. She was strongly of the opinion that it was the gentleman's place to await the lady but Sarah would not hear of such an idea.

"It really is the limit. I have to waste the whole morning acting as gooseberry to you and that French ninny when I was all set to go fishing with Tom," complained Edward.

"But, Edward, surely your father ordered you to beach your boat."

"I did, but that doesn't stop me going out in Sam's fishing smack. If Father is not prepared to trust my word then I'm damned if I'll respect his wishes."

She shook her head doubtfully.

"Take care, he doesn't find out, Edward. He'd be fearfully angry. Perhaps it is as well you are to come with us though I get the impression that you're not overfond of Captain Desormais."

"Namby-pamby creature! Fancy a man going on so about ladies' fallals. And did you notice all that preten-

tious 'His Royal Highness this' and 'His Royal Highness that'? Father was lapping it up but surely you must
prefer a real man like Tom?"

Color heightened, Arabella declared frostily:

"You can hardly compare that boorish creature with
Captain Desormais. The Captain is a gentleman."

"Gentleman? Effeminate milksop!"

Quickly recovering her composure, Arabella turned a
laughing face toward him.

"I can see the Captain has certainly not made a favorable impression on you, but surely it's too early to make
up your mind about him?"

Edward ignored this. Brows knitted, he said slowly:

"I've an odd feeling that I've seen the coxcomb somewhere before. I wish I could remember where."

"Probably in Brighton last season. He said that he was
there."

"No. It was recently but I can't recall where."

"Never mind. It's hardly important. Ah, here comes
the Captain at last."

Edward watched balefully as Captain Desormais cantered towards them on a showy chestnut.

"All done up like a dog's dinner. You can imagine
what that fancy outfit would look like after a day's
hunting. I bet he's one of those chicken hearts who leave
the field after the first fence."

To Edward's mind there could be few worse insults.
Arabella chuckled.

"You aren't being fair, Edward. Why shouldn't he look
his best? We are scarcely intending to go hunting today."

She moved forward to greet the Captain, confident
that today she too looked her best, in the dark olive riding
habit that set off her gleaming curls.

Captain Desormais's face mirrored his appreciation as
he reined in his chestnut.

He proved a competent horseman and a pleasant companion, refusing to allow his good humor to be affected by
Edward's scowls nor by his obstinate insistence on remaining close to Arabella's side—in complete contravention

of the commands urgently hissed by his mamma before he set out.

After an exhilarating gallop across the open downland they walked their horses gently along the narrow lanes towards the fishing village below.

Sam's tiny cottage lay on the outskirts. As they passed by, Arabella could not resist a glance over the hawthorn hedge. She was furious at herself for the sudden rush of disappointment when she saw no trace of Tom.

Then as they rounded the bend in front of the cottage, they encountered two strolling figures—Tom, bearing on his arm a statuesque black-haired beauty. Taking in the sensuous hips and billowing curves of bosom, Arabella decided nastily that this female would be decidedly fat before she was forty. But she was forced to acknowledge, with a spasm of irrational jealousy, that his companion's voluptuous contours seemed very much to Tom's taste. Instinctively Arabella reined back her mare, unwilling to attract Tom's attention.

Edward, less inhibited, rode forward calling a cheerful greeting. Tom tore his gaze from the raven-haired charmer.

"Hello there, Edward. We missed your help this morning." He glanced past the boy and bowed with exaggerated respect. "Your servant, Miss Ridware."

Arabella acknowledged the greeting with a cool nod then bestowed a particularly warm smile on Captain Desormais. She was astonished to catch an expression of black rage crossing his face. Before she could hazard a guess as to its cause, the look had vanished. One haughty eyebrow raised, her companion asked disdainfully:

"A friend of yours, Miss Ridware?"

Arabella bit her lip, unsure of how to answer. Out of the corner of her eye, she watched Tom pluck a rose and tuck it into the girl's bodice. She laughed provocatively up at him. While Arabella hesitated, Edward glanced mischievously back at her, with an extravagant:

"Our preserver, no less!"

She shot him a look of pure exasperation and hastened into airy explanation.

"The fellow gave us some assistance when we were in difficulties with Edward's sailing boat, some weeks ago."

Fortunately the Captain was not sufficiently interested to ask for details. Arabella rode past Tom, acutely aware of his mocking scrutiny.

"And his companion? You know the rustic beauty?"

"I've never set eyes on her before," Arabella replied shortly, conscious of a strong desire never to see her again.

Edward, who had stopped for a brief word with Tom, now drew back alongside them and butted in:

"She's Sam's sister—Grace. She lodges with Sam at the moment."

"Indeed! They must be very tight packed in that minute cottage," commented Arabella coldly.

"I shouldn't imagine Tom minds being at close quarters with Grace. She's a real stunner, isn't she?"

"Edward, I must beg you to remain silent if you cannot refrain from vulgarity."

Edward totally ignored the priggish reproof. As a sudden thought struck him, he burst out:

"That's where I saw you before, Captain Desormais. Last week—you were down on the shore with Grace."

The chestnut side-stepped nervously as the Captain's hands tightened on the reins but he quickly controlled his mount.

"I? You are mistaken. I've never seen the wench before."

"But I'm positive . . ."

"Edward, pray don't be such a bore. I don't wish to hear another word about the female."

Arabella was still furious with herself for that momentary rush of jealousy when she saw Tom's laughing response to the invitation in Grace's provocative eyes. What was it to her if Tom did admire Sam's shapely sister? Grace was his social equal, a suitable mate for him. Arabella had no excuse for interest in him so why should she feel that ridiculous twinge of envy? The sooner they forgot about Tom and Grace the better.

Deliberately she set out to be charming to Captain Desormais but to her annoyance he was oddly quiet and inattentive. Was it pique because he suspected her of harboring an interest in Tom or anger that Edward refused to accept his denial?

She remembered that half-seen flash of anger when they first saw Tom and Grace. Was the Frenchman jealous too? Was there in fact some justification for Edward's claim but, if so, why did the Captain deny all knowledge of Grace? Whatever the reason for his change of mood, the easy companionship between them was lost.

At the park gates, Captain Desormais drew out a pocket watch and regarded it regretfully.

"I fear, Mademoiselle, that I must leave you here. I am required at the Pavilion this evening. I trust that I may be granted the pleasure of your company again very soon."

Not at all convinced of the verity of this suddenly recollected engagement, Arabella nodded stiffly. With a few further compliments the Captain rode away.

Edward watched after the trim figure till it disappeared.

"I'm positive it was that fellow I saw with Grace. He was riding that flashy chestnut too. Why should he be so anxious to deny it?"

"I'm sure I don't know nor care either," snapped Arabella crossly and distinctly untruthfully.

As she pulled off her riding habit in her room, she puzzled fruitlessly over the whole problem. She was decidedly curious to discover the connection, if any, between Captain Desormais and Sam's attractive sister and more anxious to know the precise relationship between Tom and Grace, although she was not ready to admit, even to herself, that there was any reason other than curiosity behind her interest.

5

When Captain Desormais next dined with them he was as ardently attentive to Arabella as on his original visit and she began to wonder whether she had imagined that cold withdrawal. Had her own disturbed feelings communicated themselves to her sensitive suitor? For suitor he clearly was.

As yet he had made no declaration but his manner led them all to believe that he was serious in his attentions. As his visits grew more frequent, Joseph was in daily expectation of being solicited by the Captain for Arabella's hand and Charlotte had already settled the details of her wedding gown. As for Arabella, she reveled in the admiration of so gentlemanly a suitor. The Frenchman presented an agreeable contrast to the elderly wooers previously furnished by Joseph.

At theater, concert, dinner, he was her constant companion. Seemingly the Prince had relaxed his former exacting demands on his aide's time. Arabella was delighted with his companionship and the moderation of his suit. She was not yet sure of the extent of her feeling for the Captain. As an escort and friend she delighted in him but she was not certain whether she desired him as a husband. For such an intimate relationship, good humor and attentiveness were not sufficient. Much as she appreciated Captain Desormais as a companion, she was not yet in love with him.

So she was thankful that he did not seen anxious to force her into any hasty decision. Just as coolly as she did, the Captain ignored Joseph's ponderous attempts to bring matters to a head.

Luckily Joseph's attention was diverted to the organization of the local Volunteer Corps. Joseph had become a Captain in the troop led by Sir George Leyton and, tak-

ing his responsibilities very seriously, spent long hours
drilling and exercising with his men.

Edward, too, had been forced to enroll among them—
the most unwilling of volunteers under his father's command.

"They're nothing but a rabble of pot-bellied nincom-
poops,' he complained bitterly to Arabella. "Sir George
is so crippled with the gout he can barely mount his horse
and there's scarcely an able-bodied man in the whole
bunch. They wouldn't stand an earthly chance against
Bonaparte."

But a volunteer he had to remain and gloomily he rode
off with his father each day. As did the majority of the
male servants.

"I'm sure I don't know, Joseph, how you expect me
to keep this household in any sort of order," complained
Sarah bitterly, "nothing can be done properly when half
the staff is playing at soldiers for the greater part of the
day."

Her protests went unheeded. Footmen, grooms, even
Monsieur Dubois, the chef, continued to prepare to withstand the enemy whose invasion was daily more confidently expected.

One afternoon in August, Joseph came home from a
conference with his Colonel in a state of great excitement.

"There is to be a grand military parade on the downs,
in September. The Prince of Wales will review the troops
and he has invited the Volunteers to send a contingent."

"Whatever put that crazy notion into his head?"
Edward was less impressed.

"Sir George told me that His Royal Highness insists,"
Joseph's vast chest swelled in gratification, "that the gallant patriots who come forward to serve their country in
her hour of peril, are as worthy of his notice as the men of
the regular army."

"What fustian!" declared his son scornfully but, perhaps fortunately, his words went unheard as Charlotte
pressed forward, plump hands clasped imploringly.

"Oh Papa, please may we go with you to see the Review? It would be so thrilling. Please!"

Gratified by her enthusiasm, Joseph good humoredly gave his consent and arrangements were made for them all to attend the spectacle.

Joseph pressed Captain Desormais to join their party but the Frenchman regretted that he was unable to accept the offer. As a member of the Prince's household he would naturally be expected to attend the review with his royal master. He hoped, however, to spend some time with them if His Royal Highness gave leave.

"I only hope the weather is fine," Sarah's was the only despondent voice, "you know what the rain does to your rheumatism, Joseph."

A week of fine weather preceding the great day encouraged her to be a little more optimistic:

"If only it lasts . . ."

Then, on the day of the review, they awoke to find everything shrouded in mist.

"There what did I tell you," fretted Sarah. "The weather has broken. This nasty fog always gets on Charlotte's chest and her poor papa will be too stiff to sit his horse."

Impatiently Edward reassured her:

"It's only a heat haze, Mamma. It'll be a fine day later on."

Sure enough, as the sun rose higher, the mist cleared to reveal a day as fine as any in midsummer. Far from contenting Sarah, this only shifted the grounds for concern. Now she started to fret lest it should prove too hot.

"Enough to give you all sunstroke standing there in all this heat. Charlotte, my love, make quite sure that you remember your parasol, otherwise your complexion will be utterly ruined."

"A bit of sun couldn't do her much harm. She's as red as a lobster already," commented Charlotte's ungallant brother. Charlotte burst into noisy tears that only dried when her exasperated father threatened to leave her behind altogether unless she stopped her wailing. She ceased abruptly and hurried to complete her toilette.

The whole household was in ferment. Joseph bustled around attempting to hurry them all up but succeeding merely in getting in everyone's way. Between heat and agitation, his face soon took on a hue as bright as that of the resplendent scarlet coat of his volunteer uniform.

The precise design of this uniform had been the product of much deliberation. Finally, Joseph and Sir George had settled on gold-trimmed scarlet jackets, white breeches and huge helmets of black japanned leather topped by a magnificent plume of snowy white feathers. The final decision had been so long delayed that it had been feared that the uniforms would not be ready in time for the review but by dint of a heroic effort on the part of the tailor they had been delivered late the previous night.

Joseph stamped from room to room, hindering everyone and absentmindedly setting down his gloves or gigantic helmet, then dispatching all the women servants to search for them.

"With that great expanse of red, the enemy will certainly have an ample enough target to aim at," murmured Edward to Arabella, as his father strutted past them. Her smothered giggle attracted Joseph's notice.

"What are you dawdling there for, Edward?" he snapped irritably, totally forgetting that he had forbidden his son to depart without his permission. "Time you had those horses on their way or they'll be too blown to join in the parade."

Edward was to ride in advance with Jem, the groom, leading Joseph's horse, leaving Joseph to follow with the ladies. The coach would convey them to the downs beyond Brighton where the review was to take place.

Hurriedly Edward took his leave, glad to be safely out of the confusion. After a great deal more commotion, the rest of his family squeezed themselves into the coach. Even then there was ten minutes' further delay when Sarah discovered that she had forgotten her smelling salts.

"You won't need smelling salts," spluttered her exasperated husband but she declared herself totally unable to face the prospect of a day without them. A bevy of servants was dispatched on the hunt and finally the dainty bottle was discovered in her dressing room. Relieved, Sarah slipped it into the door pocket where it remained unused for the rest of the day. At long last the coach moved off.

As they drew closer to the site of the review, the road grew more crowded till at last it was completely choked with vehicles of all description, from high perch carriages to farmers' carts, all packed with passengers. A steady stream of pedestrians threaded their way through the confusion.

"We'll never reach the damned place in time," groaned Joseph, "I knew we should have started out earlier. What's holding us up now?"

Charlotte leaned perilously far out of the window.

"It's the mail coach trying to come past in the other direction. It can't get by the landau in front of us and the driver won't give way."

She giggled coyly as a buck in a nearby gig called a saucy greeting.

"Charlotte, pull in your head immediately. Such vulgar curiosity is most unmaidenly," snapped her mother.

Reluctantly Charlotte obeyed. Their coach lurched gradually forward as the mail, insisting on its legal right of way, inched slowly past them, cheered on by a crowd of urchins.

"For Heaven's sake, shut that window, Charlotte," spluttered Joseph as a cloud of dust blew in. Arabella was thankful that Sarah's gloomy prophecies of bad weather had caused Joseph to abandon his plan for using the open carriage. Hot and airless it might be, shut in here with the windows tight closed, but at least they would not arrive coated in the dust thrown up by the teeming traffic.

It had been a hard decision for Joseph to agree to use the old-fashioned coach rather than his dashingly modern barouche, designed by the Prince's own coach builder, but Sarah's nagging had prevailed. Arabella had no doubt that both Sarah and Joseph would impress upon their acquaintance that this was only their second vehicle.

She shifted slightly to avoid the great plumes dangling from Sarah's gauzy turban.

"In honor of His Royal Highness," Sarah had coldly declared them to be, when her husband rudely demanded why she was decked out like a damned peacock. As if, thought Arabella censoriously, the great helmet he was nursing was not equally ostentatious. Idly she wondered how anyone could possibly fight with such a monstrous weight on his head, then, more soberly, prayed that the necessity never arose for her to discover the answer.

They were all glad to clamber out when the coach pulled off the road on to the green downland turf. Edward was anxiously awaiting his father's arrival. Joseph immediately hurried off to where the rest of the volunteers were assembled in a wild confusion of men and horses.

"There, if he hasn't forgotten his silly hat, again," sighed Sarah.

"I'll take it to him," Arabella seized it and walked over with Edward to where Joseph was gradually sorting out his volunteers.

"Thank God we have the Navy to protect us from a French invasion," muttered Edward, watching his father's desperate attempt to produce some sort of order from the chaos, "I'd hate to imagine what this hopeless crew would do in an emergency."

Arabella watched Jem heave Joseph's great bulk into the saddle.

"Your fellow volunteers certainly appear far from warlike."

"More belly to most of them than belligerence," agreed an amused voice and she spun around to find Tom at her side. She glared crossly at him. Why did he have to appear again just when she had convinced herself that she was forgetting him.

"At least," she declared cuttingly, "however inefficient they may be, they have enough feeling for their country to volunteer to defend her."

"But Miss Ridware, you wrong me. I too don my uniform and drill with my pike in the churchyard. Alas we humble foot soldiers were not needed at the review today."

Arabella wished that he would not smile so disturbingly. It was hard to remain cool when his nearness made her pulses throb so alarmingly. She forced herself to be calm.

"It is a pity that you do not display a greater loyalty in other ways. What is the use of preparing to defend your country when you continue to betray her by secretly trading with the enemy?"

"That's just Father's nonsense," objected Edward but she shook her head. Sober reflection had convinced her of the justice of Joseph's comments on the smugglers. Pompous Joseph might be, but in this matter his condemnation was justified.

"He's right, Edward! Think of that spy they captured in Dover last month. The report stated that he had been landed from a smuggling vessel."

Hazarding a glance upward, she found Tom gazing gravely down at her. His voice came low and earnest.

"I cannot explain but please believe I am no traitor."

Then he turned abruptly and left her.

Slowly Arabella made her way back to the coach, thoughts in a whirl. She found it impossible to analyze her feelings. Common sense told her that she should have nothing further to do with Tom but somehow, when he was near, she forgot common sense. Her instinct urged her to trust him but could she depend on instinct against all the evidence? Why should it matter so desperately whether or not he was trustworthy?

"There you are, at last, Arabella. We've been looking everywhere for you."

Sarah brushed aside Arabella's apology.

"Come along. We must find a good position where we can see everything. How I wish we had a gentleman to escort us. I had hoped Captain Desormais might come but I suppose he is busy with the Prince."

They made their way to a spot where they could see the entire parade ground spread out below them. A slight breeze had sprung up relieving the heat of the bright sunshine.

Already a small crowd had gathered but there was room for everyone to have an uninterrupted view. Enterprising peddlers, bearing great trays of fruit, gingerbread and knick-knacks, moved among the throng crying their wares.

A ripple of excitement passed through the crowd as

they caught the sound of distant music. A loud cheer went up as on to the green space below them, marched orderly ranks of infantry led by a fife and drum band. Wheeling smartly, they came to a standstill facing the crowd. There was a gasp of admiration from the spectators as the magnificently arrayed dragoons cantered past. Their gold laced jackets glistened richly in the bright sunshine and the great fur crests on their helmets tossed proudly as they rode by.

"Aren't they superb?" breathed Charlotte, her lips parted in wonder.

Sparkling harness chinking, the dragoons rode into well-disciplined ranks alongside the scarlet-coated foot soldiers.

Finally the volunteers took the field. Their ragged formation came as somewhat of an anticlimax after the orderly precision of the dragoons but their loyal supporters greeted them with an encouraging cheer. Edward, in the rear, looked young and slight, jogging between two corpulent yeomen. His face bore a faintly embarrassed scowl as if he were ashamed to be involved with such a disorganized display.

The white feathers, topping the volunteers' helmets fluttered bravely in the light breeze as, without too much confusion, they jostled past the regular troops to their position at the far end of the parade ground. There they attempted to keep their restless horses under some sort of control—no easy task with mounts unused to the bustle and noise of military occasions.

Watching the harassed volunteers Arabella suddenly felt proud that they should be there, proclaiming their readiness to stand alongside the professional soldiers in the fight against the threatened invasion. Despite their faintly comic appearance and sad lack of military precision, she had no doubts that they would fight valiantly to defend their homes and families.

After some minutes had passed with no further action, the crowd grew restless.

"What are we waiting for?" demanded Charlotte impatiently.

"For the Prince, of course."

There was a bustle at the far end of the ground, and a

large barouche drawn by six horses drove slowly past the assembled troops.

"It's Mrs. Fitzherbert," came the whisper among the spectators.

Arabella gazed fascinated at the plump figure who sat in the barouche, graciously acknowledging the cheers of the crowd. She had never before seen this lady who was reputed to be the Prince of Wales' true wife. Although Mrs. Fitzherbert's religion prevented her from ever being acceptable as his legal wife and future Queen of England, it was widely believed that he had married her in secret, some years before his official wedding to Caroline of Brunswick. For a while they had parted but now that the Prince seemed irrevocably separated from the Princess of Wales, he had become reconciled publicly with Mrs. Fitzherbert.

Plumply pretty, with soft blond curls framing a sweet pink-complexioned face, Mrs. Fitzherbert sported as magnificent a set of feathers as Sarah's. They danced in the breeze as she nodded and waved to the crowd.

A loud peal of trumpets caused all heads to turn back once again as, on the field, trotted a huge grey charger bearing the Prince of Wales. Staring awestruck at the gigantic personage, whose rich blue jacket was positively smothered in gold lace, Arabella could appreciate why the unkind referred to the Heir Apparent as "the Prince of Whales."

"Doesn't he look stupendous?" gasped Charlotte.

"Truly incredible," agreed Arabella unsteadily, watching almost unbelievingly his ponderous progress along the lines of troops. Under his huge fur crested helmet the Prince looked hot and uncomfortable. The vast chest, on which glittered the jeweled garter star, heaved painfully as he panted his way among his troops.

"Look, Charlotte, His Royal Highness is stopping to speak to your papa," cried Sarah and Charlotte squeaked in excited ecstasy. Even at this distance they could distinquish the deep flush of gratification on Joseph's face at this unexpected honor.

Arabella giggled at a sudden irreverent thought.

"If poor Joseph swells much more with pride he'll burst out of his jacket and spray poor Prinny with buttons."

"Hush, Arabella! Your brother has every right to be proud of such distinguished notice."

His inspection completed, the Prince rode across to where Mrs. Fitzherbert's carriage stood. The soldiers marched smartly off the parade ground and prepared to present a mock battle. The volunteers were not required for this, so Edward and Joseph hastened to join their family.

"Oh Papa," squealed Charlotte as soon as Joseph came within earshot, "fancy the Prince speaking to *you!*"

"Yes indeed. I felt greatly honored."

"What did he say, Papa?"

"His Royal Highness was so affable as to remark that it was a dam . . . an exceedingly hot day."

Catching Arabella's eye, Edward almost burst with suppressed mirth. Recovering slightly, he whispered:

"Did you see what a massive pair father and Prinny made? If either of them gets any fatter we'll need to take a leaf out of Hannibal's book and mount our troops on elephants."

Captain Desormais now joined them and begged leave to take Arabella on a tour of the sights. With Edward and Charlotte following, they strolled through the crowds.

Although the Captain was as elegantly turned out as ever, Arabella could not restrain a slight spasm of envy when she saw the proud faces of other girls squired by red or blue coated heroes. A civilian, however modish, seemed somehow second best today. With the faintest hint of reproach she declared:

"I thought to have seen you in uniform today, Captain Desormais."

"No, Mademoiselle. I assumed you knew that I had sold out. Though of course, should the threatened invasion materialize, I should re-enlist and fight alongside my old companions."

"Henri, you dog, no wonder you've been avoiding us all lately. Want to keep this pretty filly to yourself, eh?

Introduce me or I'll force payment on all your notes of hand."

Captain Desormais frowned, as a heavy hand descended on his shoulder. Reluctantly he turned.

"Miss Ridware, may I present Sir James Lengton, another member of His Royal Highness' household."

"Servant, Miss Ridware," Sir James' flushed countenance betrayed that he had been drinking. "This your heiress, Henri? Don't know how you manage to sniff 'em out."

The Captain tried to move away but his embarrassing friend grasped his arm confidingly.

"Just saw 'nother friend of yours, Henri. All the pretty girls love Henri!"

"Quiet, James, you're foxed! You'll embarrass Miss Ridware."

"Not a bit of it. Black-maned filly. There she is."

Following the direction of his wavering finger, Arabella recognized the shapely form of Grace. The girl was talking intently with a short gaunt man but glancing up and seeing their eyes upon her, she tossed her head arrogantly and walked away.

Captain Desormais scowled at his friend.

"You're talking nonsense, James. I don't know how you manage to get so disguised this early," he declared lightly and drew Arabella firmly away. Sir James' raucous laugh followed them.

"Don't want the pretty heiress to know about Grace, eh, Henri?"

Only the slightest flush betrayed Captain Desormais' annoyance. His voice continued light and unruffled:

"I must apologize for my friend, Miss Ridware. I fear he was sadly intoxicated. Please pay no attention to his foolish words."

Arabella could not help but be perturbed by this second linking of Grace's name with the Captain's. She could not altogether blame the Frenchman if he had been attracted to Grace, who was undoubtedly a beautiful creature, but Arabella wished that he would be honest and admit that he had at some time been associated with her. This obstinate denial seemed so unnecessary.

Smiling down into her troubled face, Captain Desormais cried playfully:

"Such a serious frown, Mademoiselle. You must cheer up before we meet His Royal Highness."

"The Prince . . . you mean . . ."

"To present you to my royal master. But of course, Mademoiselle."

She stared at him, wondering why this was the first time he had mentioned it. Had he really intended to surprise her or was this a spur of the moment decision—an attempt to make her forget his friend's thoughtless disclosures? Impatiently she rejected such a suspicion as fantastic.

Heart throbbing, she walked beside Captain Desormais, to where the Prince stood beside the barouche which had brought Mrs. Fitzherbert. The corpulent figure beckoned graciously to them. She curtsied deeply in acknowledgment of his creaking bow as Captain Desormais smoothly made the presentation.

Close to, the Prince of Wales was indeed enormous but, gross though he appeared, some remnants of the charm that had so enchanted society in former years, still showed. The fairy-tale Prince Florizel had coarsened into Prinny but his personality still had enough force to disarm and captivate. He took Arabella's hand in a moist grasp.

"This is indeed a pleasure, Miss Ridware. I can appreciate now why Captain Desormais has been neglecting us all so shamefully these past weeks."

As she murmured a disjointed disclaimer, he caught sight of Charlotte wriggling excitedly behind her.

"And this charming young lady, Miss Ridware? Is she your sister?"

"My niece, Miss Charlotte Ridware, Your Highness."

"Charlotte!" The bulging eyes moistened. "Namesake of my own sweet child. How she would have loved to be here today. Desormais, you must bring these charming young ladies to one of my evening parties. I'm sure you will enjoy it Miss Ridware. Bring Miss Charlotte—and that gallant young fellow with her—Desormais will make all the arrangements."

He nodded an affable dismissal and struggled up into the carriage beside Mrs. Fitzherbert. Arabella moved back, overwhelmed by his unexpected friendliness—that impulsive familiarity which the high sticklers among his acquaintance so deplored.

Charlotte had to be prodded by her brother before she followed. As they forced a way through the crowd surrounding the royal party, a sudden uproar made them start around.

A short wild-eyed man was running towards the Prince, his arm upraised. Even as Arabella realized that the object he brandished was a pistol, she saw the great figure of Tom launch himself upon the puny fellow.

As they fell together, a shot rang out. Transfixed with horror, Arabella breathed, "Tom—no—not Tom."

Dimly she was aware of the barouche lurching and the Prince falling back in his seat but anxiety for Tom so filled her mind that she did not register the significance of the movement till Charlotte screamed:

"The Prince! He's shot the Prince!"

6

Arabella put a tremulous hand on Captain Desormais' sleeve. Raising frightened eyes to his, she was puzzled by the odd glow in his dark eyes. Was it anger or triumph that blazed momentarily there? Before she could decide, the expression was gone, leaving only understandable concern for the Prince.

The Captain shook off Arabella's hand and hastened to join the crowd milling around the barouche where the Prince lay sprawled, with Mrs. Fitzherbert bent anxiously over him.

Relieved to see that at least the Prince was still alive, Arabella threaded her way back to where a subdued Charlotte and Edward watched the fallen heir to the throne.

The Prince struggled into a more dignified position, then stood upright to prove to everyone that he was un-injured. The sudden shot, it now appeared, had startled the horses, unseating their royal burden. The pistol ball had passed over the Prince's head and he was suffering only from shock.

All attention now swung a little to the left where, in the center of a seething knot of people, Tom had hauled the would-be assassin to his feet. Surveying the small battered man, Arabella's eyes widened in sudden remembrance. Surely this was the gaunt individual she had seen talking with Grace? All his former fervor had been knocked out of the undersized fellow and he limped dejectedly away, each elbow grasped by a sturdy dragoon.

Angry boos and hisses followed him. A few missiles were thrown—most of which hit the burly dragoons not their captive.

The noise died away as the Prince of Wales raised his hand. The normally high color had drained from his face, and his plump hands trembled slightly but with an effort the Prince regained his poise. His voice was reasonably steady.

"My friends, I trust that this incident will be swiftly forgotten by you all. No harm has been done and I would not wish that any word of it should come to the ears of my royal parent. He, too, has lately suffered murderous attempts from misguided extremists. Thanks to the prompt action of that brave fellow there, the attempt was foiled and I beg that you all forget it was ever made."

His voice quavered slightly on the last words and he sat down abruptly. Mrs. Fitzherbert, leaning forward, patted his plump hands and spoke softly. He nodded and, beckoning one of the grooms, pointed at Tom who had turned and was trying to move away from the excited mob surrounding him.

Reluctantly, Tom allowed himself to be led to the side of the barouche. The Prince leaned out to shake him warmly by the hand and Mrs. Fitzherbert added her gentle but obviously heartfelt thanks.

Among the throng beyond the barouche, Arabella caught a glimpse of Grace's raven tresses. The girl's dark eyes glittered tempestuously, her face bore a scowl as black as that with which Captain Desormais surveyed the hero's reception afforded Tom.

Edward's sharp eyes had spotted Grace too.

"Look at Grace over there—sick as a cat over all the fuss Tom is getting!"

Arabella raised a questioning eyebrow.

"I thought you were one of the lady's admirers. Why this turnabout?"

"Who me? Not likely! She's too dashed free with her favors for my taste. Wants all the men dancing attendance. It's not just Tom. There's Joe from the King's Head always hanging around after her and Jem. I've even seen Dubois making sheep's eyes at her."

"I'm sure I saw her talking to that man who tried to shoot the Prince."

"I wouldn't be at all surprised. Nothing in breeches is safe from her. Sam and his wife are just about fed up with

her. They wish to goodness she'd go back to Shoreham
but there was some sort of scandal she came to avoid and
they have to put up with her till it's blown over. I don't
mind so much about the others but I hate to see a decent
chap like Tom made a fool of. Look there she goes to
butter him up."

Arabella was horrified at the stab of jealousy she ex-
perienced as Tom warmly responded to the provocative
dimpling smile with which Grace greeted him. She turned
abruptly.

"Come Charlotte, Edward, we must get back to your
parents. They'll be wondering what on earth has happened."

But even as she moved determinedly away, Arabella
could not resist one backward look. Across the heads of
the crowd her glance met Tom's. His eyes crinkled in that
familiar teasing grin and he half lifted one hand in greeting. The other arm was flung carelessly around Grace's
shoulder.

Disdainfully Arabella tossed her fiery curls and swung
her parasol up to block off the infuriating sight. It mattered not a whit to her if Tom was bewitched by that
swarthy peasant, she told herself vehemently, and quite
untruthfully.

Weakly she ventured another glance back, with even
less satisfaction. Already Tom had forgotten her and was
totally engrossed with Grace. Miserably Arabella followed
Charlotte and Edward. Charlotte, desperate to tell her
parents about the thrilling events, hurried ahead and burst
into excited speech as soon as she reached them:

"So awful, Mamma. A wild monster of a man—he
rushed up with a pistol to shoot the Prince, and a man
knocked him down. The Prince fell and we thought he
was dead. Everyone screamed! I thought I should die of
shock! Then some men took him away—the man, that is,
not the Prince. *He* was all right and . . ."

Arabella stood silent while Joseph and Sarah tried to
disentangle their daughter's confused tale. She remembered, shamefaced, that moment of guilty relief when she
imagined that the Prince had fallen victim to the assassin's

bullet, not Tom. It was deplorable but her first concern had been for the tall smuggler. Charlotte's frightened cry had proved almost reassuring.

Already Charlotte had remembered the even more exciting news.

"Captain Desormais presented us to the Prince, Mamma," she squealed. "And only guess, he—the Prince that is—has invited us to the Pavilion. Isn't it thrilling?"

For once the peevish frown vanished from Sarah's face. Captain Desormais, appearing opportunely, was plied with eager questions. For which day was the invitation? Who would be there? What should they wear?

The Frenchman answered with polite resignation. As soon as he could extricate himself, he made his way to Arabella's side.

"I have to apologize, Mademoiselle, for leaving you so abruptly but I knew you to be in the capable care of Master Edward."

The speed with which she had been abandoned, when Edward was far from close, still rankled with Arabella but she accepted the Frenchman's apology graciously.

"I quite understand, Captain Desormais."

"So formal still, Mademoiselle? Please call me Henri. Then I will know myself forgiven."

"Very well—Henri. I trust that you left His Royal Highness fully recovered."

A frown darkened the Frenchman's face.

"Yes, perfectly. He was fussing over a reward for that uncouth yokel."

"Uncouth . . . You mean Tom?" spluttered Edward. "If it had not been for him, the Prince would have been killed."

"I very much doubt it. The fellow over-dramatized the whole incident in order to impose himself on His Royal Highness. The other poor creature had obviously no real intention of firing. His pistol went off by accident in the shock of the sudden attack by that burly ruffian."

"Nonsense," but Edward was forced to relapse into angry silence as his father brusquely ordered him to hold his tongue.

Arabella was surprised by the petulant way Captain Desormais referred to Tom's actions. Could it be caused by jealousy, she wondered—of Tom's valor or his conquest of Grace? Whatever the reason, she was disappointed by the Frenchman's ungenerous attitude and found it impossible to respond with her customary warmth to his assiduous attentions.

For a fortnight after the review, nothing was spoken of in Ridware Hall save the Prince's evening party. The impressive gilt-edged invitation cards had pride of place on the mantel and Sarah smugly pointed them out to any caller who might conceivably have overlooked them. To his relief Edward had not been included in the invitation. He and Captain Desormais were in a state of armed truce, so his name had been omitted when the latter drew up the list but Sarah, Joseph and Arabella's own mamma had been included.

Captain Desormais' assistance was canvassed on the most suitable attire for them all. For once, Sarah generously engaged the Brighton designer who fashioned her own gowns to sew those of Charlotte and Arabella. Not so munificent a gesture as Sarah pretended, for Arabella's mother, though steadfastly refusing to join the party, quietly offered to pay for both girls' outfits. An offer which was immediately—and just as unobtrusively—accepted.

Madame Thérèse drove out to Ridware Hall bringing patterns, materials and trimmings for their inspection. She brought, too, something of which Arabella had heard but which she had not seen before—a set of wax dolls clad in miniature replicas of the latest styles.

Charlotte's younger sisters, tempted from their nursery to discover the cause of all the commotion, fell on these dolls with shrieks of delight. Sympathetically Arabella watched Madame Thérèse hovering anxiously, obviously wondering how she could rescue her precious models without offending their doting mamma.

Fortunately, before they could do much damage, Sarah, tiring of their squabbles, packed her unruly daughters back to their nurse with the totally false assurance that

Madame Thérèse would bring them a pretty doll apiece on her next visit.

Arabella and Charlotte fingered the fine fabrics and pored enthralled over the pattern books before they eventually made the difficult choice.

Madame Thérèse worked quickly and very soon returned with the garments ready for fitting. This time her daughter came to help her. Arabella was highly diverted when, in an effort to put the bashful young assistant at her ease, she tried a few words of French on her. The girl stared in baffled incomprehension.

"I'm sorry Annette, I presumed you to be French like your mamma."

"Lor no Miss! Ma's not French neither. Plain Emma Clay, she is, only the hoity-toity lady visitors from London don't think no one English can make gowns like them Frenchies."

Then, conscience stricken, she looked awkwardly at Arabella, obviously regretting the frankness that the girl's friendliness had tempted her into.

"You won't let Ma know I told you, Miss? She don't like it known that she's never been nearer Paris than Dover Harbor."

"I won't breathe a word—not even to Mrs. Ridware." Particularly not to Sarah, she added inwardly, Sarah being a typical example of those foolish females who despised anything English. She patriotically hated the French nation *en masse,* but eagerly embraced their fashions and manners.

Sourly, Sarah watched as Charlotte and Arabella paraded for her approval.

"No, Charlotte, you really cannot have any more ribbon on that bodice. Arabella, that neckline is far too revealing."

"But Sarah, everyone wears them like this."

"Perhaps they do among the underbred hoydens of the demi-monde. A lady should be more modest. It must be altered."

Resignedly, Arabella stood while the shoulders were pinned to raise the bodice, ruining the delicate line of the

simply cut gown. But though the demure Annette pinned
in obedience to her mother's directions, plain Annie Clay
whispered reassuringly in Arabella's ear:

"Don't fret Miss, Ma'll pull all these pins out when
we get home. She don't let folks ruin her reputation with
their silly whims."

Shrewdly, Arabella suspected that Sarah's irritability
was caused by her dismal failure to make Charlotte look
at all presentable in the sickly pink creation the girl had
set her heart on.

Arabella slipped off her own simple, silver-threaded
white muslin, and left Sarah trying to persuade Charlotte
to leave off a little of the over-elaborate trimming.

A little later, her quiet stroll in the shrubbery was interrupted as Charlotte panted up.

"At last I've found you. Mamma wants to see you at
once."

"What does she want?"

"I don't know but do hurry! She's as cross as a crab
already."

Arabella followed her back into the house, vainly
searching her conscience. She must, she finally decided,
be guilty of some sin of omission as she could remember
no recent misdemeanor. Though one rarely knew what
Sarah would take offense at.

Her face was certainly stormy.

"You've taken your time coming, Arabella."

Arabella answered soothingly:

"I'm sorry for the delay, Sarah. I was in the garden
and had to change my slippers before I came upstairs."

"Never mind. You are here now. I require your help,
Arabella."

Arabella stared suspiciously at her.

"My help?"

Her sister-in-law afforded her a thin lipped smile.

"Yes, Arabella, your assistance. You will probably
have noticed how very spotty Charlotte's complexion is
becoming."

"Oh, Mamma!"

"There is no occasion for that vulgar outcry, Charlotte. The truth must be faced, however unpalatable."

It was Arabella's private conviction that Charlotte's complexion had been ruined by the excessive quantities of sweetmeats she gorged but charitably she kept this opinion to herself, merely asking:

"How can I be of any help, Sarah?"

"I wish you to take Charlotte to bathe in the sea at Brighthelmstone tomorrow."

Charlotte gave a horrified wail.

"Bathe—at this time of the year! It'll be freezing!"

"I should certainly not suggest such a step in any other conditions, Charlotte. Dr. Earlswood assures me that, although it is extremely unwise to bathe when the body is heated and the waters warm, at the present time of the year, immersion can be very beneficial."

Not in the least enthusiastic about the idea, Arabella forced herself to smile warmly at her sister-in-law.

"It sounds an excellent notion, Sarah, but would it not be better if you accompanied Charlotte yourself? The bathing might relieve those headaches you suffer so."

Coldly, Sarah corrected this hopeful suggestion.

"On the contrary, Arabella, Dr. Earlswood says that excellent as the practice can be for such afflictions as Charlotte suffers from, it would not at all suit in my case."

Crestfallen, Arabella reflected that she might have guessed as much. Dr. Earlswood's popularity with her sister-in-law originated in his willingness to agree with whatever pronouncements Sarah made about her, largely imaginary, maladies. Without much hope she tried a final protest.

"Couldn't one of the maids go with Charlotte. She'd be far handier to help . . ."

"Certainly not! Of course, Arabella, if you are determined to be disobliging, I am sure your dear Mamma would be willing to go in your place."

"That won't be necessary. I will go."

Sarah smirked triumphantly at the success of this ploy.

"Very well then. The coach will be ready tomorrow at eight. Edward will go with you both."

Yawning, the reluctant trio set out next morning, accompanied by a disapproving Mollie. Edward rallied a little when he discovered Jem at the reins. He climbed on to the box and persuaded Jem to let him handle the ribbons.

Even with the most determined use of the whip he could not rouse his father's sedate team to the speeds coaxed from their thoroughbred cattle by the Brighton bloods but he managed a better pace from them than the poor creatures had ever before attempted.

His inexpert driving made the journey even rougher than usual. Charlotte, never a good traveler, grew steadily whiter. Mollie drew out the foot rest to try and make her more comfortable, but she looked really queasy by the time they reached Brighton.

"Well the worse she is, the more there'll be to cure," was all the sympathy afforded by her brother.

"Are you going to bathe too, Edward?" Arabella interrupted Charlotte's noisy recriminations.

"Not likely! I've more sense. If I want to swim I do so off a quiet beach not in one of those wheeled monstrosities. I'll see you back at the coach in an hour."

Secretly, Arabella agreed with his views and regretted that it was impossible for a female to behave so unconventionally. She and Charlotte must suffer the use of a bathing machine.

Reluctantly they scrunched their way across the beach to where stood the drab wooden cabins on wheels. A stout red faced woman greeted them cheerfully:

"Come along, dearies. Don't be frightened. Old Bess will take care o'you."

A second woman pushed between them.

"Sea water dearies? Do you a power o' good."

Hesitantly they took a glass each. After a tentative sip, Arabella, revolted, put hers back on the tray but a shuddering Charlotte bravely drained the glass.

"Aren't you coming with us?" she wailed when Mollie handed them their towels and bathing dresses.

"No, Miss Charlotte, you don't get me to leave dry land. T'isn't natural to go messing in that nasty water."

"Come along Charlotte! Let's get it over."

Impatiently Arabella pushed the younger girl up the wooden steps into the damp hut. A small window high up on one side let in sufficient light for them to see the hard wooden benches on each side and a sprinkling of wet sand on the floor.

Shivering with cold and apprehension, they began to tug off their clothes. Charlotte shrieked in terror as, with a jerk, the whole structure began to move.

"What's happened?"

"It's only the horse pulling us down to the sea."

"Oh, Arabella! I've dropped my stays on the floor."

"Well pick them up, you goose, before they get soaked."

Arabella pulled the shapeless dark flannel bathing dress over her head and tied the strings round her waist and ankles, then turned to help Charlotte fasten hers. The bathing machine lurched to a standstill and Bess' gruff voice called:

"Ready, dearies, out you come then."

She opened the door and they stood hesitantly on the threshold, surveying the uninviting greyness of the heaving waves.

Fully dressed, the dipper stood waist deep in the sea.

"Go on, Charlotte!"

Arabella gave the girl an impatient push forward. As Charlotte balanced on the bottom step, the burly dipper seized her and dumped her bodily under the waves. Her shriek of alarm turned to a choked gurgle as the water closed over her terrified head.

Quickly Arabella ran down the steps and plunged determinedly into the water to avoid a similar forced ducking. At the first shock of immersion, her warm flesh recoiled from the coldness but soon her body adjusted and she splashed about happily. The long trailing robe hampered her movements but she enjoyed the sensation of floating. Dimly she heard Bess' gruff voice above her, admonishing Charlotte.

"Come along, Missie, see how brave the other young lady is."

But Charlotte struggled wildly to the bathing machine

steps and clung shivering there, refusing to be tempted
back into the sea. Teeth chattering, she turned her gaze
shoreward. Tittering she called to Arabella:

"Look, Bella. Those impudent fellows are watching us
with a telescope from up there."

"You take no notice o' them dearie. Bess'll make sure
they don't annoy thee. Tis only their low idea o' fun."

Indeed the huge female dipper looked a match for any
overbold gallant but Charlotte continued to stare ashore,
giggling:

"Aren't they awful, Bella!"

Arabella frowned at her. If Charlotte had learned nothing of real value in three expensive years at Miss Scropton's Academy, she had managed to acquire an embarrass-
ingly coy and oncoming attitude towards young men.

"Charlotte, for goodness sake, stop staring at them.
They'll imagine you want to encourage their insolence."

Charlotte took no heed.

"Look, Bella, surely that is your Captain Desormais
over there. It *is!* Talking to a pretty, dark-haired girl. Do
look Bella."

"Certainly not." Flushed, Arabella scrambled out of the
water, pulled Charlotte into the hut and slammed the
door.

In silence they rubbed themselves dry. A brisk toweling
soon restored the circulation to Arabella's goose-pimpled
limbs and she dressed herself as best she could while the
sturdy horse dragged the swaying bathing machine up the
beach, then she turned impatiently to help Charlotte. The
girl's greeny pallor alarmed her.

"Are you all right, Charlotte?"

"Oh, Bella, I feel dreadful."

"It's that sea water. You shouldn't have drunk the whole
glassful."

"I know—and I swallowed a lot more when that horrid
creature pushed me under."

When they finally emerged from the bathing machine
they found Mollie waiting anxiously. She seized the wet
towels and bathing dresses, scolding gently:

"Look at you both shivering. I don't wonder at it neither. T'isn't natural to go messing in all that nasty cold water."

Charlotte stumbled and clutched at her stomach.

"Oh Mollie, I feel so sick!"

"Just you come along Miss Charlotte. We'll look after you, don't you fret."

Arabella stared around, then pointed:

"There's an inn just along the road. We'll have to take her there to rest. She couldn't stand that bumpy coach yet."

Before they reached the inn, a cheerful voice hailed them. A former schoolfriend of Charlotte's, passing with her mother, had seen them cross the beach. Shocked by Charlotte's pale wretchedness, they insisted that she be taken to their nearby cottage.

"Unfortunately we have only the one guest room, Miss Ridware, but I am sure we can find room for you, too, somewhere."

Arabella thanked them but declined the offer.

"I had better go home to explain to my sister-in-law. Edward will look after me."

The friends hurried off to prepare for Charlotte's reception while Mollie guided her slow progress behind them.

"I ought to come with you, Miss Bella. I can't leave you alone in this wicked place."

"Don't be foolish, Mollie. The coach is only along the road. Edward will be waiting there. I'll be quite safe."

Mollie still looked dubious but concern for the now ashen Charlotte forced her to remain with the invalid, and reluctantly she allowed Arabella to depart.

With less assurance than she had pretended, Arabella hurried to the quiet road where they had left the coach. She was much later than the time they had arranged and hoped that Edward would not have grown tired of waiting.

The vehicle was drawn up by the roadside, horses already harnessed. It looked oddly deserted. The horses moved restlessly. One had twisted awkwardly catching

himself up in the traces. With difficulty she straightened
him. She stood talking soothingly to calm them, hoping
they would not take it into their heads to move off. Her
frail strength would never restrain them. Fortunately
Joseph's team were mild enough creatures, though as she
clutched convulsively at the leader's bridle, they caught
some of her nervousness and fidgeted uneasily.

Arabella looked around in anxious perplexity. Where
was Jem? It was most unlike him to leave his horses unattended. And where was Edward?

She scanned the quiet road. It was empty save for a
bearded man who plodded wearily towards her. One empty
sleeve was roughly pinned to his loose fitting jacket.

Arabella shrank back in alarm as the shabby figure
ambled closer and halted beside her. Then she gasped in
startled relief as an unexpectedly jovial voice greeted her
from out the tangled beard.

"In trouble again, Miss Bella? Can I help?"

She peered disbelievingly at him.

"Jack? Is it really you?"

"None other, Miss."

"But your poor arm! What dreadful accident has happened to cause that?"

The ruddy bearded face crinkled into a pleased grin.
With a swift glance around, he bent closer.

"Nothing at all, Miss. See!"

With a roguish wink, he pushed a stout tanned fist out
from the folds of his vast jacket.

"But why?"

He laughed at her startled expression.

"'Tis safer this way, Miss, when the press gang's in
town. A man with only one hand is no use to the Navy
so they leaves me be."

"The press gang? Could they have taken Jem? He was
supposed to be here with the coach but there was no sign
of him when I got back here."

Jack nodded soberly.

"Very likely, Miss. They're supposed to take only sea-
faring men but they'm none too fussy in wartime. Any
strong young lad will do."

A sudden chilling thought struck at Arabella. She gaped in sick horror at him:

"Edward! He was here too—all unsuspecting. Pray God they have not taken him!"

7

Jack put a comforting hand to pat Arabella's shoulder.

"Don't fret, Miss Bella. T'isn't so likely they'd press Master Edward. They knows tis too risky to meddle with the gentry."

Arabella tried to believe him. But although his words were reassuring, the concern in his weathered face told another story. Obviously, Jack had his doubts too. All the same, she admonished herself severely, panicking would do no one any good.

A servant emerged from the house opposite. Jack hailed him:

"Hey, you there! Have the press gang been along here?"

"Aye, they have, half an hour ago, rot 'em. Took our stable boy and the lad off that coach there. Put up a good fight he did but they dragged him off poor devil."

"Ask him about Edward," urged Arabella.

"Did you see a young gentleman took too, about fifteen, slim, dark-haired?"

The man shook his head.

"Didn't see no one like that but I didn't hang around to watch. Didn't want to be took meself, did I? I hopped it quick. Sorry I can't help you, Miss."

Arabella had to be content with this faintly hopeful report. She tried to stay calm but the dreadful fear that Edward might be in the hands of the press gang was not easily dispelled.

Jack surveyed her anxiously.

"What'll you do now, Miss?"

"I suppose I must try to discover for certain what has befallen Edward. If he really has been seized then I must go back to Charlotte's friend, but I must find out."

"I'll go and see if I can get word of Master Edward anywheres in town, Miss. Do you want to come with me?"

After a second's thought, Arabella shook her head.

"No. If you search I had better wait here in case he does turn up."

Jack stood hesitating, conflicting emotions working in his face. Finally:

"Are you sure you'll be all right, Miss Bella? I don't like to leave you here on your own but some of the places I'll be trying are scarce fit for a lady."

Arabella smiled faintly and assured him that she would be perfectly safe.

"If you'd be so kind as to help me unharness the horses before you go, I can sit quite comfortably in the carriage."

"Aye that'd be best. They look as if they've stood too long already."

It was not a task with which either of them was familiar, and Jack's strapped up arm made it even more awkward, but eventually they had all four horses securely tethered and grazing on the grassy road edge.

Jack helped Arabella into the coach, then set off waving a brief farewell with his free hand. Despite her brave assurances, Arabella felt horribly forlorn as she watched his stout form disappear down the road. He had slumped forward once more, his gait reduced to an infirm shuffle. If she had not seen him working beside her, agile and active, only a few minutes before, she could readily imagine him at death's door.

Now that she was again alone, her spirits plummeted. Huddled in a corner of the coach, she turned the problem over and over in her mind.

Surely Edward must have returned to the coach by now if he was still at liberty. Could Edward have deliberately put himself into the path of the press gang? She knew how bitterly he resented his father's refusal to let him join the Navy. Could he have seized this opportunity to achieve his ambition?

Yet Arabella could hardly believe that he would choose such a way. Edward had always wanted to become an officer like his grandfather and pressed men entered as ordinary seamen. Life below deck would hardly suit Edward.

But she could not be sure. Perhaps for Edward, even life as an ordinary seaman would be preferable to remaining idle at home. Men had risen from the ranks to command their own ships. Could Edward have seen this as the answer to his problem and deliberately courted impressment?

A sudden shouting and commotion in the distance roused her from her troubled brooding. She peered curiously out of the window but there was nothing to be seen.

The shouting came again, louder, closer, this time. Her anxious ears caught the sound of heavy footsteps approaching. For a moment she hoped this was Jack returning but no—his had been a slow shuffle; these footsteps pounded towards her, heavy and ominous. She pressed clammy hands tightly together to stop them trembling and shrank further into the corner hoping that whoever was outside would pass by without noticing her. The footsteps faltered as they drew closer and the whole coach lurched violently as a heavy body slumped against its side. Her heart thumping painfully, Arabella peered out.

"Who—who's there?"

"Your servant, Miss Ridware."

The answer came feebly and Arabella stared aghast at the swaying figure that raised a weakly mocking hand.

"Tom! What's happened to you?"

"Press gang. Almost got me. I gave them the slip but they won't be far behind. I must hurry."

Even leaning against the side of the carriage he could scarcely stand. Arabella scrambled down and tried to support him but his weight was too much for her to bear unaided. She had to let him slide gently to the ground. Falling on her knees beside him, she saw a great bruise already turning blue on his forehead and a thin trickle of scarlet blood running from a nasty gash beside it. She stared wildly around but there was no hope of assistance in the deserted road.

The distant shouting grew louder—the sound of running

feet closer. The press gang? Arabella looked doubtfully at the slumped figure.

"Can you manage to get to that house opposite if I help you? The servant there was helpful."

Tom shook his head wearily.

"No. It's too late. We'd never make it before they arrive. Leave me here. I don't want you involved in all this."

With sudden resolution, she contradicted him firmly:

"Nonsense! Of course I must help you. It'll have to be the carriage. Get inside and on the floor. It won't be comfortable but it's better than being pressed."

He grinned with a ghost of the familiar mockery.

"Better squashed than pressed, eh? You're very kind, Miss Ridware, but . . ."

Arabella stamped an exasperated foot.

"Don't be ridiculous! You can't give up now! Hurry and get in."

He was too weak to argue further. With the last remnants of his strength he stumbled up the creaking steps and lay on the floor of the coach. Arabella climbed up behind him and slammed the door shut.

"Anyone looking in would see you there. Try to get as far under the seat as you can."

Try as he might, Tom could not force his broad frame any further under the low seat.

"The foot rest!" Arabella seized it and Tom squeezed himself half under the seat, half under the foot rest. Arabella sat and spread her slim skirts. For the first time ever, she wished that fashion still favored the ample garments popular when her mother was young. Their billowing folds would hide anything. With the tubelike muslin skirts now fashionable, it was a far more difficult task but she did her best with them.

It was a far from satisfactory arrangement but she was confident that, at least, Tom was hidden from a casual glance. She prayed that no one would give more.

They were ready not a moment too soon. As Arabella sat up, straightening her straw bonnet, the press gang burst around the corner.

The two leading men brandished cutlasses. Behind them others wielded ugly cudgels. The sickening memory of similar cudgels striking relentlessly on to the heads of the excisemen thrust uncomfortably into Arabella's mind.

She had tried to forget it—imagined the whole episode over—yet here she was, again helping Tom to evade capture. Not that he was in such deadly danger this time. Service in the Navy was hard and strict but it was not so grim a fate as hanging. For a brief second Arabella wondered if she was doing the right thing. Might Tom not be safer as a sailor than continuing to risk his life running cargoes ashore?

Then she remembered the bloody wound on his head inflicted by one of those brutal weapons and she determined to preserve him from another such blow.

She shook with inward terror as the young officer halted beside the coach. He saluted her politely.

"Beg pardon, Ma'am. Have you seen a man come along here? A tall man, wounded he'd be."

Arabella forced herself to smile winningly at him.

"A great overgrown fellow you mean, lieutenant? Yes, indeed. He ran past here, not three minutes ago—down towards the beach there I think."

"That'll be the one we're after. Thank you, Ma'am."

Some demon inside Arabella tempted her on. She fluttered long lashes.

"Why lieutenant, what has he done? He looked a truly villainous creature. I was terrified!"

She ignored the faint quiver of amusement from beneath her and fastened green eyes on the young sailor's face. He gulped bashfully:

"Resisting impressment, he was, Ma'am, but we'll get him, never you mind. No need for you to be alarmed."

"Hurry, you fool, or you'll miss him!"

Startled, Arabella swung around to see from where those venomous words came. On the other side of the road she recognized the raven locks of Grace. A hectic spot burned in each cheek as the girl glared at the lieutenant.

Grace's anger was patently genuine but why should she be so anxious for Tom's capture?

"Don't worry. You'll get your bounty sure enough."

The officer's voice was icily contemptuous.

"This way, lads."

He saluted Arabella briefly and signaled his men to proceed along the road. Grace set off impatiently before them. Arabella breathed a sigh of relief that Grace had not recognized her. A second band of sailors now caught up with the first. They led a string of bound captives. No Edward, but Arabella spied the disheveled figure of Jem. Impulsively she cried out:

"Jem, are you all right?"

As he turned painfully, she saw the great livid bruise on his temple and called furiously after the officer:

"What have you done to my groom? You have no right to take him. He's no sailor."

The lieutenant halted his men and turned embarrassed.

"I'm sorry Ma'am. I'm only obeying orders. Our information is that all these men have served at sea."

"Is that true, Jem?"

"Yes, Miss Ridware. Six months in the Navy when I was fourteen. I had to give up when my ma took ill. Captain Ridware gave me a job in the stables and I got to like that as well as the sea."

"But how did they find out about it so long ago?"

She followed his bitter glance to where Grace impatiently awaited the press gang.

"Grace?"

"Yes, Grace, that's who told 'em," his voice rose angrily. "Grace indeed. *Disgrace* would be more like it. Selling her friends for a few miserable coppers. Even Judas asked silver!"

The faintest deepening of Grace's color betrayed that she had heard but she did not even glance in his direction. Again she called harshly to the lieutenant:

"Hurry, you fool, he'll get away."

As soon as they had gone, Arabella bent anxiously to see how Tom was. She was shocked at how ill he appeared. The crimson trickle across his brow accentuated the ashen pallor of his face. She mopped ineffectually at it with a handkerchief.

"I'll have to get help from one of these houses."

"You can't. They'll be back immediately they see I'm not on the beach."

She searched for something more substantial than the lacy wisp of handkerchief to mop his wound, and remembered her lawn tippet. She ripped off a long strip to bind around the wound. Before she had time to fix more than the most rudimentary bandage, an approaching clamor heralded the return of the press gang. Regretfully she helped Tom squeeze back into his hiding place.

The frustrated fury on Grace's face delighted Arabella. As the angry girl stalked past, she looked straight up at the carriage. Smoldering dark eyes met cool amused green and Arabella saw recognition dawn in Grace's face. Triumphantly the girl shouted:

"Stop you idiots! He's there—in that coach."

Arabella set her teeth and determined to brazen it out. She was a match for this vulgar creature. Whatever Grace's reason for betraying Tom, Arabella was not going to let her succeed.

Arabella opened wide green eyes in injured innocence.

"What does she mean? Here? The poor creature must be deranged."

"Don't listen to her, you dolt. She's his fancy woman. Would a proper lady be sitting there all on her own?"

Still he hesitated. Arabella did not have to feign her indignation at this insult. She addressed herself with icily controlled fury to the young officer:

"Am I to be blamed because my coachman has been dragged off by your brutal ruffians? I have made no complaint about it although the man was savagely injured and my horses left all unattended. Heaven knows what harm they might have suffered! My maid has gone to find someone to drive us home and you insult me for waiting here. Do you expect me to traipse all over town?"

"She's lying! Look inside and you'll find your man."

As the officer looked unhappily from one angry face

to the other, Arabella decided to hazard everything on a bold bluff. With immense dignity, she rose.

"If you really imagine that your wretched felon is here, I suppose I am obliged to permit you to search but I cannot think what my brother will say. He is busy with Sir George Leyton at present, arranging our defenses against the French. They will both be furious when they learn how abominably you have insulted me. Still if you insist I suppose that I *must* come down and let you search. Make sure that you do no damage or I'll not answer for the consequences."

As she had anticipated, mention of the magistrate's name caused the young officer to pause. She waited, nerves stretched unbearably. She could feel Tom's tension. For an endless minute everything hung in the balance, then, Grace thrust forward.

"I'm not scared of her threats! Let me look. I'll soon drag him out."

The young lieutenant pushed her aside. His expression was unhappy but he declared firmly:

"It's my place to search not yours. If you would be so good as to step down, Ma'am, I'll not trouble you more than a moment. I know the man is not there but it is my duty to look."

Arabella realized that she had failed. Slowly she opened the coach door.

There was a wild shriek and around the corner panted a bedraggled female, grubby skirts held high. A scruffy mob cap half covered her tousled locks. She grabbed at the officer's arm, gasping:

"Quick, Mister, 'e's back there—Tom Knighton—'e's in the Grinning Monkey. Landlord sent I to tell you. 'Urry!"

She sank breathless onto the grass. The lieutenant looked vastly relieved. He rapped out an order and his men set off at a jog trot.

"Wait for me!"

Grace darted a look of angry malice at Arabella and chased after the press gang.

Arabella stared in incredulous suspicion at the gawky

servant girl. It could not be—but yes—as the last sailor disappeared around the bend, the newcomer stood jauntily up and Edward's dark eyes twinkled merrily at her from under the mob cap.

"Quick Bella! Help me with the horses. It's quite a way to the Grinning Monkey but they'll be back as soon as they find Tom's not there."

As she jumped down from the coach, Jack hurried to join them.

"He's safe in there, is he, Miss?"

"Tom? Yes, he's in the carriage but he has a nasty head wound."

"Make sure he stays inside, Miss Bella. I'll help Master Edward with the horses."

She turned to find that Tom had indeed struggled up and was swaying weakly in the doorway. Concern made her scold sharply:

"Get back inside at once! You'd only be in the way."

He acknowledged the truth of this and sank wearily back. His wound needed attention but that must wait. Arabella reluctantly left him and ran to help with the horses.

Edward had often helped in the stables and he soon had the team in place. Arabella breathed a sigh of relief as she scrambled up into the coach again. There was still no sign of the press gang returning. She could hear a friendly tussle on the box where Jack and Edward struggled over the reins.

Edward won and with a jolt that threw her sharply back they moved away. Beside her Tom lay palely against the cushions, his eyes closed. Even the wild pitching as the coach hit a massive pothole failed to rouse him completely. He stirred faintly, muttering:

"Wild weather. Get the headsails in. Fire as you will."

Surely those were Naval terms? Her eyes widened as a new thought pressed in. Had Tom been in the Navy already? A deserter? God knew there were many of them. No wonder he should be so anxious to avoid the press gang!

He tossed agitatedly. She must try to calm him or the

movement would open up his wound. If only she had something to help rouse him.

Then the memory came of Sarah calling for her smelling salts and slipping them into the door pocket. Arabella rummaged inside and drew out the cut glass bottle. She waved it gently under Tom's nose.

"Tom! Wake up! Tom!"

He stared drowsily at her.

"Arabella? What in the world . . ." as consciousness returned a teasing twinkle animated his eyes. "Smelling salts. Very auntlike!"

"They're not mine. Sarah left them in the pocket," snapped Arabella irritably. The coach jolted once more and Tom winced painfully.

"Whoever is driving this vehicle?"

"Edward."

"Yes, I suppose it isn't quite bad enough to be Jack. I'll need to give young Edward some lessons."

She eyed him uncertainly. Teach Edward to drive? Where would Tom have had the opportunity to learn himself? Was his mind still wandering?

His eyes had closed again. She felt his pulse—steadier now. This seemed a more natural sleep. Carefully she slipped a cushion behind his head. Lying back, defenseless, Tom looked suddenly much younger, more vulnerable.

The coach lurched violently again, throwing her off balance. Tom was jolted too, his arm flung out and clasped her waist steadying them both. Afraid to disturb him by drawing away, she did not move. The arm tightened and drew her closer.

Tired by all the excitement, she rested thankfully. It seemed perfectly natural to nestle her head into Tom's shoulder. She savored the stolen moment—after all, Tom was asleep. No one would ever suspect her weakness.

All too soon, the coach jerked to a standstill and she heard Jack climb down.

"We've arrived at Sam's, Miss Bella. We'd better drop Tom off here."

She pulled herself free. With a faint sigh of regret, Tom

set her gently upright. Arabella flushed hotly. How long had he been awake? Indignantly she hissed:

"You imposter! I thought you were asleep."

"No. Just too comfortable to move."

He smiled disturbingly as the warm flush spread. There was an electric tension between them; she waited breathless but Tom turned away as Jack's anxious face peered in at them.

"You all right, Tom?"

"Yes, thank you. Miss Ridware has been tending me most charmingly."

"What in Heaven's name were you doing to run foul of the press gang?"

Edward pushed his way past him, into the coach.

"He came to help me. I was just going into the Three Tuns when the gang arrived and they nearly grabbed me."

Arabella stared at him, brow creased.

"The Three Tuns. Why that's nothing but a smuggl . . ." her voice trailed off awkwardly as she realized her blunder.

"Don't mind us, Miss Ridware. It is as you say—a low smugglers' haunt. I don't know how many times I've warned Edward to keep away. Next time I'll tan his hide for him."

Edward grinned unrepentantly at him.

"I had to see you. Warn you the gang were after you."

"And in the process nearly get yourself *and* me packed off to sea. Thank you very much. Shouldn't you be looking after those poor unfortunate horses?"

"Sam's holding them."

"But how did you know the press gang were after Mr. Knighton?" interrupted Arabella.

Edward raised an eyebrow at this dignified address.

"I heard Grace telling your Captain Desormais while I was watching you bathe."

"Watching . . . Edward, you are a revolting creature!"

"Not half as revolting as that sister of mine. She looked like a great blue whale emerging out of the sea. I must say you're a better shape!"

Arabella glowered speechlessly at him, trying to ignore Tom's chuckle of appreciation. Edward went on:

"Where is Charlie anyway? Did you drown her?"

"Of course not. She drank too much sea water and was sick. Mollie took her to the Dunsters' and I came to find you. I was really worried when I got to the carriage and found you gone and Jem."

"I know. They got Jem, poor devil. I'd have been with him now but for Tom."

"And no more than you deserve, neither, Master Edward," declared Jack severely, "putting Tom in such danger!"

"I must own it would have proved a trifle awkward to be pressed."

"Awkward! You'd not be joking if . . ."

Tom frowned warningly and Jack's grumble died away. Had her suspicions been correct then, wondered Arabella. Was Tom a deserter? It did not fit somehow with her idea of him. Dominant, lawless, infuriating, the smuggler might be, but she could not imagine him deserting. Yet how was she to know what pressures there were on a man in the Navy? Some of the tales her father had told, made her secretly sympathetic towards those desperate sailors who had mutinied six years ago. If Tom was a deserter he must have a valid reason.

While she pondered she heard Jack ask:

"Did you say you saw Grace with that prissy Frenchman, Master Edward?"

"Yes, she was creeping along so furtively that I followed to see what she was up to. She told him she'd lead the press gang to Tom."

Jack nodded triumphantly:

"Perhaps now you'll agree I was right about that damned female. Same trick as she played before. Got all the lads mad for her then sold 'em for sailors. You can't say no one warned you!"

"Ah yes, Jack, but she was such a tempting armful!"

The laughing words were addressed to Jack but the teasing sidelong glance was for Arabella. She bristled indignantly but remained silent, determined not to betray the jealousy that suffused her.

"But what has Captain Desormais to do with it all?" puzzled Edward.

"I'm not sure . . ."

"Nothing! Surely he is just amusing himself with that wretched female like the rest of you!" snapped Arabella crossly.

"More than that, he seemed to be giving her orders."

"You're imagining it. You try to put the blame on Captain Desormais just because you don't like him."

"Bella! You cannot really admire that French booby."

"He is not a booby! Because he takes a pride in his appearance is no reason to deride him."

"Surely you don't mean to marry him, Bella?"

Arabella glared at him.

"Why shouldn't I? Not that I shall marry anyone till I'm asked but when I am, I will not require your permission. Now it's time we were getting home. The horses have stood for far too long."

She nodded coolly as Tom began a teasing speech of farewell.

"Please don't waste time thanking me. You should be having that head attended to."

That reminded Jack of Tom's hurt and, concerned, he led Tom into the cottage. Edward, still grumbling, climbed back on to the box.

Arabella settled back in dismal isolation. Let them imagine her in love with the Frenchman, if they wished. Why should Tom be the only one to have other irons in the fire? If he supposed that she minded about his silly flirtation with Grace, he was very much mistaken. Captain Desormais, with his respectful consideration for her wishes, was far more to her taste than any arrogant smuggler.

Defiantly she told herself that she was glad that Jack had interrupted that vibrant moment when she had felt sure that Tom was about to kiss her. Jack had merely saved her the trouble of smacking Tom's face. It was only the prospect of explaining to Sarah the unfortunate details of her trip to Brighton that was making her feel so low . . .

8

Once home, Edward drove straight around to the stable yard. The elderly coachman hobbled out to meet them.

"Where's that idle varmint Jem got to, Master Edward?"

"Pressed!" Edward replied tersely, uncomfortably aware of the grinning delight of the stable lads as they took in the hilarious details of his feminine garb.

"Pressed for a sailor? Serves the poor wretch right. Wheedling me to let him take my place so he could meet his sweetheart in town. I warned him no good'd come of it. Well, it'll be a long day afore he sets eyes on her again. Took back into the Navy he was always hankering after. Just when I had him trained too. Have to start breaking in another dratted lad—worse trouble than the horses they be!"

Still grumbling he trudged across to help Arabella alight.

"Hope the poor beasts haven't taken no harm from Master Edward's handling. Too wild with 'em he is!"

"I'm sure that if he has overtaxed them, they will soon recover under your excellent care, Bliston."

He snorted his contempt of this patent attempt at pacification and bent anxiously to examine his precious horses' legs.

Arabella hurried away. Just outside the yard, Edward hovered impatiently awaiting her. She rounded crossly on him.

"Are you mad, Edward! All the boys were laughing at you. Why ever didn't you get rid of those ridiculous garments before you reached home?"

He glared back.

"Don't you think I would have if I'd had anything to change into? Jack wouldn't let me keep my own clothes

93

underneath in case they showed. I left them at the Three Tuns."

That reminded Arabella of her earlier anxiety.

"You seem very involved with all these smugglers, Ned. Are you sure it is wise?"

"Oh Lord, Bella, don't you start! I have enough from Tom. He's always on at me to stay clear of them."

"Very wise advice."

"Damned hypocritical if you ask me. He's in the thick of it. Why try to warn me off?"

Unwilling to accept the logic of this argument, Arabella temporized:

"Perhaps he cannot help himself. He has no other way to earn a living. You have not that excuse."

"For Heaven's sake, Bella, stop the moralizing! I'll take care. What I want to do now, is get indoors and out of these revolting petticoats."

They made their way, in strained silence, to the side door. There Edward hesitated.

"Be a love and go first, Bella. See if the coast is clear. If Mamma sees me in this pickle, I'll never hear the last of it."

For a moment she glared at him then capitulated. It was difficult to stay cross long with Edward.

"Very well, this once."

Gloomily aware that her own appearance, though less exotic than Edward's, hardly conformed to Sarah's exacting standards, Arabella cautiously opened the door.

A soft cough made her spin guiltily around. Hamstall stared impassively at her.

"Beg pardon, Miss Arabella, but Mrs. Joseph requested that you and Miss Charlotte attend her in the drawing room immediately you return."

"Thank you, Hamstall. I will do so as soon as I have changed my gown."

Her attempt to sneak upstairs was frustrated by a steely voice.

"Is that you, Arabella? Come here, at once."

She had no choice but to obey. Sarah was comfortably disposed on her sofa, embroidery in hand. Arabella fidgeted uneasily as her horrified sister-in-law took in every detail of her disheveled appearance.

"Why are you so disgracefully late, child, and where is Charlotte? I informed Hamstall that I wished to see both of you immediately you returned."

"Charlotte has not come home. She was unwell so Mollie took her to stay with Sophy Dunster."

"Unwell? Charlotte?" Sarah stared incredulously at Arabella, then gave a tink shriek of alarm, "Arabella! Is that blood on your sleeve? What has happened to my poor child?"

Arabella looked at her sleeve which indeed still bore evidence of her attempts to tend Tom's wound.

"Oh no, Sarah! This isn't Charlotte's blood!" frantically she tried to think of some acceptable explanation.

"I—I—must have scratched myself—on the bathing machine, the wood was very rough." Aware how thin this excuse sounded, she hurried on, "Charlotte was upset by the sea water she drank and I was afraid the motion of the carriage might make her really ill. You know how prone she is to travel sickness."

"Travel sickness, poppycock! The child has far too much imagination. Fancies herself unwell for no reason."

"She takes after you . . ." Arabella faltered, thinking better of the impulsive retort. She wondered uneasily if she had been too rude this time but Sarah, after staring hard at her, decided the comment was merely inane.

"Quite the reverse! Charlotte is fortunate enough to have inherited her papa's robust constitution. It was totally unnecessary to trouble the Dunsters. I'm sure they cannot afford to entertain guests. They're as poor as church mice. Not that the Dunsters would have anything to do with the church. Methodists, I believe!"

From the scorn in her voice, she might have been accusing them of being devil worshipers.

"I could hardly refuse. Charlotte seemed so unwell and they were so pressing in their invitation."

"Leaving you to come home alone. Most unladylike! Surely, Arabella, you could have sent a message by the coachman instead of gallivanting around the countryside in this hoydenish fashion, all alone."

"I had Edward to accompany me."

Before the words were out of her mouth, Arabella realized her error.

"And where pray is Edward?"

"I—I—think he's getting rid of his dirt . . ."

The soft murmur of Edward's voice in the hall gave the lie to this statement. Arabella exclaimed brightly:

"There's a most unpleasant draft here. I'll close the door before you catch a chill."

"That is quite unnecessary, thank you. Leave it open."

Arabella shook her head warningly as a tattered Edward crept towards her, ready to slip past when his mother's attention was focused elsewhere. Sarah's eagle eye caught the faint movement. She sat up calling imperiously:

"Edward! Come in here! I wish to speak to you."

Abandoning all hope of concealment, Edward caught up his ragged skirts and fled.

With a hysterical screech, Sarah fell back on to her cushions, eyes closed. Arabella moved instinctively to assist her, then, thinking better of the impulse, turned and tiptoed to the door. Once roused, Sarah would demand an explanation. Let Edward make his own excuses for once.

A surprisingly vigorous voice from the prostrate figure on the sofa, halted her retreat:

"Where do you think you are off to, Miss?"

"I thought I'd fetch your maid . . ."

"It may have escaped your notice but all the rooms in this residence are furnished with a bell to summon the domestics. No—not now, girl, I have no desire to be mauled about by that dithering imbecile. What I require is an explanation of Edward's preposterous appearance."

"He had to disguise himself to avoid the press gang."

"Press gang?"

"Yes. In Brighton this morning. They dragged Jem off the carriage most brutally and Edward feared they might attempt to capture him next so he put on those clothes to deceive them."

"I have seldom heard such ridiculous nonsense. The impressment officers take Edward indeed. Surely the foolish boy knows that my brother would prevent any such absurdity. Jonah has a most responsible position at the admiralty and he—I really cannot see what you find so amusing, Arabella."

Arabella, who had been unfortunately struck by the singular inappropriateness of such a name for anyone in the naval service, humbly begged her pardon and escaped quickly to her own room.

She contrived to avoid Sarah for the rest of the day. That evening, as she scrambled into her new figured muslin, she recollected with relief that Captain Desormais was expected to dine with them. His presence should prevent Sarah's dwelling further on the day's misfortunes.

Dressing for dinner proved slow and awkward without Mollie's deft assistance. Arabella cursed the long row of tiny buttons fastening the back of her gown but eventually she had them all done up.

It needed several attempts before her hair looked anything like presentable. Luckily fashion favored a casually disordered style and she hoped that any untidiness would be attributed to artistry not lack of skill.

Tugging on pale kid slippers, she hastened downstairs to join the rest of the family in the drawing room. Captain Desormais had already arrived and moved forward to greet her with a winning smile.

"At last, Mademoiselle, but such a charming appearance is well worth waiting for. That delightful hairstyle is new, is it not?"

Edward, returned to conventional garb, looked challengingly across at the elegant Frenchman.

"We wondered if we would see you today, Captain Desormais. We feared you might have fallen victim to the press gang."

The Captain stared coldly at him.

"I? Certainly not! They know better than to interfere with members of the Prince's household."

Sarah interrupted impatiently:

"Edward has the ridiculous notion that he was in some kind of danger of impressment in Brighthelmstone today. I have assured him that my brother at the Admiralty would prevent any such error."

"My uncle's influence did not save Jem."

"The cases are not the same. Jem is not the nephew of an important official."

"I suppose if they knew of my uncle it might make some difference but they hardly ask for your family history before dragging you off. And once in their hands, it is quite a job to escape. Were you not even a trifle concerned about walking in Brighton this morning, Captain?"

"I am never apprehensive but today the problem did not present itself. Business kept me at the Pavilion all day."

"But I saw you, with Grace . . ."

"You are mistaken."

Captain Desormais was totally unruffled. Arabella looked unhappily from the Frenchman's calm countenance to Edward's scarlet-faced fury. Could the boy be mistaken? But Charlotte too had claimed to see the Captain talking with a dark-haired girl. Yet why should he lie?

Before Edward could argue further, Hamstall came to announce dinner. Glad to shelve the problem, Arabella took Captain Desormais' proffered arm and walked thankfully into the dining room. In all the rush and confusion that morning she had missed her luncheon and was now positively ravenous.

While Arabella did full justice to her helping of roast duckling, Sarah turned the conversation to the subject most in her thoughts.

"I am so looking forward to the Assembly next week, Captain Desormais. Sir George has told us of the magnificent improvements His Royal Highness has made to the Pavilion and I long to see them for myself."

The Frenchman nodded enthusiastically.

"They are indeed splendid, Madame. His Royal Highness has a rare genius for such matters, and he no sooner thinks of a new plan than it must be started at once. He is never satisfied! At Carlton House, just as here in Brighton, we are in a constant state of flux."

"How very upsetting for you all," commented Arabella.

"It certainly can be at times. The workmen seem to be permanently in residence."

"I trust everything will be ready for the evening party."

"I'm sure it will. May I help you, Mademoiselle, to a little more of this delectable sauce? Your brother's chef has excelled himself this evening. Perhaps a trifle more duckling, too?"

Arabella accepted gratefully. Not for the first time, she had been conscious of a distinct regret that Captain Desormais should consider her needs so genteely small. Her hunger was far from assuaged by the delicate morsels that the Captain deemed appropriate for a lady's portion. She looked expectantly at him as he stopped carving; he took the hint and piled a few more wafer-thin slices on to her plate, declaring:

"You are indeed fortunate, Mr. Ridware, to have found such a skillful chef here in Sussex. Of course His Royal Highness brings his chef from London but the poor man cannot prepare everything for big social occasions such as that next week. He has grave difficulty in discovering suitable pastry cooks to aid him here."

"I sympathize with him," agreed Joseph heartily, "I was extremely lucky to secure Monsieur Dubois' services. He came to me from the Comte of Marennes you know."

"Really, a Frenchman? No wonder the food is so excellently prepared. At the Pavilion we are quite in despair over our search for such artists. But I must not bore you with our domestic problems."

"If you would not consider it presumptuous of us to offer," began Sarah diffidently, "I am sure Mr. Ridware would be only too happy to permit Monsieur Dubois to give any assistance he can to His Royal Highness' chef."

Captain Desormais directed his most charming smile upon her.

"You are too kind, Madame, but I would not dream of causing you any inconvenience."

"Not at all! Not at all! Only too delighted to help out," boomed Joseph.

The Frenchman waved an elegantly resigned hand.

"If you insist, Sir, I must gratefully accept your generous offer."

"Bet he thought they'd never take the hint," muttered Edward in Arabella's ear.

"When d'you want the fellow, Desormais?"

"If you could be so kind as to let him come to the Pavilion tomorrow, he could receive his instructions. Then he would not be required again till the actual day."

"Certainly! Certainly! That will be perfectly convenient. I'll give him leave to miss the volunteer parade tomorrow."

"Ah, he forms, then, one of that gallant band. How are your troops progressing, Mr. Ridware?"

"Coming along nicely, thank you. We'll be ready for that damned tyrant, Bonaparte, when he lands."

"I am in no doubt as to the result of such a battle. You think then, Mr. Ridware, that the invasion will come soon."

"Bound to, Captain. But we'll be ready for him, never fear. When the beacons are lit, my men will all be in their places, ready to defend their homes and loved ones."

"But what of those loved ones? What is to happen to your family, Mr. Ridware, while you so gallantly engage the invaders?"

"Worried about our Bella, eh, Captain? That's all arranged don't you fret! The womenfolk are to make their way inland with the carriage and spare horses. Bella and Charlotte will ride, the rest go in the coach. They'll easily find their way to my sister at Richmond while we push those plaguey Frenchmen back into the sea."

"I can see you are well prepared though I pray the occasion never presents itself to put your plans into action."

"Amen to that," agreed Sarah with a shudder, "my flesh creeps just to think of it. How I could endure such an ordeal, I do not know!"

"Ah, but you English ladies are so calm and resourceful. I have a great admiration for you all."

Though the words were addressed to Sarah, his warm smile rested on Arabella. She was unable to meet the gaze. Uneasily, she recognized that Captain Desormais—even to herself it was difficult to call him Henri—was growing more particular in his attentions.

Sarah had noted her embarrassed withdrawal and spoke sharply when the ladies removed themselves to the drawing room:

"Modesty is all very fine, Arabella, but it is necessary to give some encouragement to a gentleman.

"If you carry on in this missish way, you'll frighten off Captain Desormais as you have all your other suitors. Do you want to stay an old maid, Arabella?"

Not if that involved spending the rest of her life in this household, thought Arabella bitterly. But was she willing to spend it with Captain Desormais either? She doubted whether, buried here in the country, she would ever receive a better chance.

Tom's image swam briefly before her eyes but she banished it determinedly. Even if he were interested in her, which she doubted, he was hopelessly ineligible. Supposing Joseph never discovered his lawless activities, he would still not consent to so unequal a match and Joseph had control of her purse strings. Captain Desormais remained her sole hope of escape from Ridware Hall.

She forced herself to respond warmly to the Frenchman's gallant greeting as the gentlemen rejoined them. Behind her she could sense Sarah purring with delight like some sleekly satisfied cat. Joseph, too, was beaming in the evident expectation of ridding himself of his troublesome ward. Well, she would be equally delighted to be released from his care.

As she finished her song, she smiled meltingly into the Frenchman's deep brown eyes. He bent forward eagerly and took her hand in his.

"Alas, I shall not be able to visit you again before we meet at the Pavilion. May I beg the privilege of leading you out in the first two dances, Arabella?"

"The pleasure will be mine, Captain . . . Henri!"

"I await the day, impatiently. If your dancing is as

delightful as your singing, I shall be indeed fortunate." He bent even closer so that only Arabella could catch the next soft spoken words.

"I trust that any offer I may make will be equally favorably received," then seeing how she blushed and moved away, he added penitently:

"But I forget your maiden modesty. You will tell me that I must speak first to your brother."

Arabella was silent, not knowing how to answer him. She indignantly resented the notion that she must be bound by Joseph's whims, yet to express that opinion might precipitate the proposal for which she was not ready. She compromised by murmuring gently:

"You go too fast for me, Henri—now let us try this new duet."

"I am delighted to join with you in any activity, dear Arabella!"

When she sank wearily into bed that night, Arabella found that despite her tiredness she could not sleep. She had staved off a proposal that evening but before she met Captain Desormais again she must decide what her answer would be. How should she decide?

She found Henri pleasant and likeable enough. A certain lack of frankness over his relationship with Grave gave her pause, but such a fault was not sufficient to damn him utterly. Men regarded such affairs very differently. Any relationship Henri had with Grace would not alter his regard for Arabella. Indeed she felt only annoyance at his obstinate denials of knowing the girl, not the raging jealously that consumed her when she saw Grace with Tom.

There was the true objection. She had not that thrilling awareness of Henri's presence that tingled through her when Tom was close. Yearningly she remembered the blissful sense of belonging there that had overwhelmed her, when she rested against his shoulder in the carriage.

Henri could not inspire such a feeling in her, but neither did he rouse such a seething resentment. Bitterly she acknowledged that Tom treated her generally like a foolish schoolgirl. He amused himself with her just as

lightly as he did with Grace. Worse still he was un-
ashamedly lawless, a criminal carrying on an illegal trade
with the French which could do nothing but harm to his
country. How could she honorably yield to an affection
for him?

Resolutely she put all thought of those mocking grey
eyes from her mind. Henri was the only choice. He loved
her. Maybe Henri might appear a less romantic figure
but she wanted her marriage to be a stable, temperate
relationship. When Henri asked her to marry him she
would say yes!

With this firm determination she fell asleep and in-
furiatingly dreamed all night of Tom.

9

When two days had passed with still no news from Brighton of Charlotte's progress, Sarah's mood passed from a
mild concern to violent rage.

"I have no doubt the foolish child is racketting around
Brighthelmstone with that flighty creature, Sophy Dunster.
Her mother never had the slightest control over that young
miss. How could you leave my poor Charlotte to be led
astray by her, Arabella!"

Remembering Charlotte's deplorably oncoming attitude
to the young bloods who had watched them bathe, Arabella suspected that Mrs. Dunster's vigilance would be
needed more on her guest's behalf than her daughter's,
but it would hardly help to share that opinion with Sarah.

"Sophy always seemed a quiet, docile girl to me," she
ventured.

"No need to bother your head over Sophy Dunster,
Mamma, she wouldn't say boo to a goose," Edward
backed up Arabella's opinion.

Sarah pursed her lips.

"So she may pretend but I am not so easily deceived.
She looks a sly piece to me; a most unsuitable companion
for Charlotte. I cannot imagine why the chit was allowed
to enter Miss Scropton's Academy—nor how her mother
managed to scrape together the fees!"

Somewhat to her surprise Edward knew the answer to
this:

"Her uncle's rich as Croesus. He manufactures something or other in Birmingham. He paid for Sophy to go to
school with her cousin, as a sort of companion."

"Trade! I might have guessed there was a nasty smell
of the shop about that family!"

"Not Sophy's side. Her papa was quite unexceptional
—younger son without two ha'pennies to rub together but

104

he starved respectably rather than disgrace his family by earning a living."

Sarah totally ignored the sarcasm. She stared with horrified suspicion at her son.

"Why are you so remarkably well informed about the Dunsters, pray?"

"Charlotte was always on about them when she started at that snobby school. If you are so worried Mamma, let me take Arabella to fetch her home?"

"Send Arabella and have another empty-headed girl join their junkets! No thank you, Edward. I will go myself with you tomorrow morning if Charlotte does not come today."

When Sarah had swept haughtily away, Arabella laughed at Edward's dismayed expression.

"Serves you right, my lad! I suppose you wanted an excuse to go after your low friends again. Your Mamma won't let you out of her sight in Brighton. She's really worried now—thinks you're smitten with Sophy Dunster."

"Good God, what put that notion in her head! I hope if I ever went overboard for a female I'd have better taste than to choose that tallow-faced mouse."

"Come now Edward, she's a pretty enough little thing if you like quiet girls."

"I don't—don't like girls at all if it comes to that. Silly brainless creatures!"

"I'd best crawl away, suitably crushed."

He grinned back unrepentant.

"You know what I mean, Bella. Aunts are different. You don't giggle around a fellow like Charlie and her friends. That makes it even more of a waste when you get mixed up with such a nasty bit of goods as that Frenchman."

He was gone before she could frame a suitable retort. It was disturbing that Edward, whose judgment she generally respected, should be so decidedly against Captain Desormais. Was it jealousy—a dislike of the Captain taking the companionship that Edward had always enjoyed —or had his keen perception really fastened on a genuine defect in the Frenchman? Whatever the reason she would be very sad if her marriage deprived her of Edward's society.

Either the sea bathing or the enforced rest in a more frugal household from overeating, had considerably improved Charlotte's complexion. Her skin, when she returned next morning, was a far better color and most of the distressing spots had vanished. Sarah, naturally, gave the credit to her farsightedness in sending her daughter to bathe. Watching Charlotte start immediately gorging sugar plums, Arabella was less certain of the permanence of the cure.

"Lor, Bella," Charlotte spoke thickly, her mouth full, "I *was* sick after you went!"

"You'll be sick again if you eat any more of those sweetmeats."

"Not I. I need them. I haven't had any for days. Mrs. Dunster don't have a sugar plum in the house. No wonder Sophy's so thin. You should have heard the impertinent remarks a young man we saw in the library made about her! I was furious with him. The odious wretch followed us right along the Steine till we met Mrs. Dunster! She soon frightened him off."

"How disappointing for you."

"Oh la, Bella, don't be so prim. We never encouraged him. I didn't even look round at him above twice."

With such artless confidences, Arabella appreciated Sarah's wisdom in fetching her daughter away from temptation but Sarah had already forgotten that worry in a greater. She poured it out at dinner:

"Mrs. Dunster tells me that in Brighton the invasion is hourly expected. It would be just like that dreadful creature Bonaparte to choose next week and ruin the Prince's evening party!"

"Surely, Mamma, not even the French would be so ill-bred!"

"You may mock, Edward, you are not invited so cannot be disappointed. I could not bear it if we were to miss the assembly."

When the great day arrived, she dispatched Hamstall four separate times during dinner, to make quite sure the

beacon had not been lit, before she dared to hope that
Bonaparte had not deliberately set himself out to ruin her
first visit to the Pavilion.

In Monsieur Dubois' absence, dinner was a scratch
meal of cold meats and pastries. No one minded the
austerity for once. As Charlotte inelegantly phrased it:

"Now we can save room for all the gorgeous tidbits
they are bound to serve at the Pavilion."

After dinner they hurried off to change into their new
clothes. Arabella was well pleased with her appearance
in the simple high-waisted gown which fell straight from
beneath her bosom to her ankles. As Annie Clay had
promised the neckline was unaltered, giving a perfect fit.

Sarah scowled disapprovingly when she saw it but said
nothing. As the long shawl slipped from her sister-in-law's
shoulder, Arabella gasped indignantly. How had Sarah
the gall to criticize anyone else when the front of her own
gown plunged so disastrously low? It was not even a
flattering display. Sarah's bosom was practically non-
existent. A string of inferior pearls twined around her
scrawny neck and disappeared among the loose mauve silk
folds of her bodice.

Joseph paced irritably up and down the hall as they
waited for Charlotte. Creaking at every step, he looked
acutely uncomfortable in an overtight dark-blue jacket
trimmed with enormous gilt buttons. An exact copy the
tailor had assured him, of the Prince's favorite design. A
vast, starched muslin neckcloth thrust up under his rolling
chins.

"Drat the girl! Where is she? We'll never get there!"

Eventually Charlotte panted downstairs to join them,
looking better than anyone had anticipated now that most
of the trimming had been ruthlessly pruned from her
gown. With her hair combed severely back, her face
seemed less pudgy. She beamed excitedly at them all.

"Don't we all look fine. La, Bella! What beautiful roses.
Did Henri send them for you?"

Arabella flushed faintly as she touched the delicate
blooms.

"I suppose that they must be from him. There was no name with them."

Sarah interrupted tartly:

"Don't be foolish girl. Of course they are from Captain Desormais. Who else do you think would be sending you flowers?"

How could she answer that, wondered Arabella. Tell Sarah that she had seen Tom give ones just like these to Grace? But she knew that Tom could not have sent the flowers. It must be a coincidence that Captain Desormais had chosen a similar bloom.

"How romantic Henri is," breathed Charlotte enviously.

As the carriage lurched slowly through the chaotic traffic all bound for the Pavilion, they peered out at the imposing new wings.

"Those fancy window decorations must have cost a fortune," grunted Joseph, eyeing the green shell-like canopies admiringly. "No wonder the Prince is always up to his ears in debt."

Inside, the Pavilion held still more architectural delights and the decorations were equally dramatic. Exotic birds, beasts and flowers wreathed everywhere in a colorful riot of Chinoiserie. Not even Captain Desormais' vivid descriptions had prepared them for so gaudy a show.

"How beautiful it all is," shrieked Charlotte as each new spectacle revealed itself. Arabella was less exuberantly approving. This flamboyant display was a little too extreme for her taste.

Overwhelmed, they made their polite bows to the Prince of Wales and Mrs. Fitzherbert. Sarah looked a little sour at being forced to acknowledge the latter but she knew well that to slight Mrs. Fitzherbert was a certain end to any hope of favor with the Prince. Like many another aspiring lady, she swallowed her pride and curtsied meekly to the plump lady.

The Prince of Wales, resplendent in dark blue coat, his buttons even bigger and shinier than those on Joseph's jacket, graciously acknowledged their courtesies and they moved on into the crowded salons.

Arabella stared around her as they forced a way through

the crush. Surely among such a throng she should recognize some familiar face but all seemed strangers. As she sank thankfully into an empty seat in a less crowded corner, she did finally recognize an acquaintance but it was scarcely one to give her any pleasure. An unctuous voice bade them good evening and Sir Giles Farnham bowed deeply before them. He ignored Arabella's cool nod and hurried to grasp Sarah's limp hand.

"Mrs. Ridware! What a delightfully unexpected pleasure. I am overjoyed to see you again!"

Sarah looked faintly surprised at his enthusiasm.

"Indeed, Sir Giles? We have not seen you this six months or more."

"My dear Mrs. Ridware, the loss was mine. Will you not introduce me to your delightful little companion?"

For a moment Sarah stared blankly at him, then she realized that his greedy eyes were fixed on Charlotte. As if, thought Arabella, the wretch were mentally stripping the clothes off her. She shuddered, remembering the embarrassment of enduring such glances herself when she was the object of Sir Giles' gallantry. Charlotte, less sensitive, tittered and stared boldly back at the baronet.

Her mother swiftly recovered her poise.

"But of course, Sir Giles. I was forgetting you had never met my little Charlotte. She was at school when you were . . . When you visited us last year. Make your bow to Sir Giles Farnham, my sweet."

Charlotte giggled and fluttered her eyelashes provocatively at the overweight baronet. Eagerly she accepted his invitation to dance, turning with exaggerated sympathy to Arabella.

"What a pity you cannot stand up with us Bella but I must not keep poor Sir Giles waiting till you find a partner . . ."

She tripped happily away smiling encouragingly at her attentive companion. Suddenly she started and let out a surprised squeak. Serves the little minx right, thought Arabella with grim satisfaction. That would teach her that Sir Giles was not one to need such oncoming smiles. He was notorious for his sly pinches and slaps.

It was hard to hear the music strike up and still have no sign of her promised partner. Reluctantly she was obliged to turn down two other invitations, then just as she was gloomily deciding that he would never come, Captain Desormais strolled across the room.

"Our dance, I believe, Arabella."

She stood up gratefully and let him lead her to join the set. As she had anticipated, he was an excellent dancer. They moved gracefully through the set. The dance movements showed off Captain Desormais' well-formed figure to its best advantage and she felt proud of having so elegant a partner, sensing the envy of less fortunate girls.

After they had danced down the set she found herself standing beside a flushed gentleman who swayed visibly as he surveyed her insolently through his quizzing glass. He slapped his thigh and laughed coarsely:

"Damn if it ain't Henri's pretty little heiress. Thought I knew the chestnut mane!"

Arabella pretended not to hear him. He swayed closer and drawled:

"Hoity-toity Miss, eh? Poor old Henri'll live under the cat's paw."

She moved away, still ignoring him but soon the movement of the dance brought her back beside him and he leaned closer.

"Has Henri popped the question, yet?"

Exasperated she snapped back:

"That, Sir James, is none of your business!"

"Don't despair, Miss Fiery Locks. He will. Poor old fellow needs the cash too much to wait much longer."

"Take care Henri does not hear your insolence," she hissed furiously, "or he will require satisfaction."

Sir James put back his head and roared with amusement.

"Henri call me out! That's a good one. You don't call out a man you owe money. Not at all the done thing!"

His raucous voice must have reached Henri but to her surprise the Frenchman made no sign of resentment. She supposed that he was unwilling to make a scene in so public a place and risk the Prince's anger.

When the dance ended Henri led her back to her seat. "I fear I must leave you now, Arabella. Even on such delightful social occasions duty calls. May I hope for another dance after supper?"

She nodded hoping that he was intending to deal with Sir James' impudence in private.

A panting Sir Giles Farnham led Charlotte back and bent amorously over her. Sarah smiled thinly at Arabella.

"It seems that your old beau finds Charlotte more to his taste now, Arabella."

"I'm sure she is welcome to him though I would wish her a younger partner."

"Come now, Arabella, no sour grapes."

An angry retort quivered on Arabella's lips but she repressed it. If it afforded Sarah any satisfaction to imagine her jealous of Charlotte's success with Sir Giles, why deny her that pleasure?

She glanced idly around the room. Her eyes widened suddenly, riveted on a tall, broad-shouldered man who stood, his back towards her, at the far end of the room. She chided herself impatiently. It could not be Tom! She was indeed in a sorry state when she must imagine every large man to be he.

A neighbor's son asked her to dance and she stood up willingly. When she got back to her seat, she saw that Charlotte was still engrossed with Sir Giles and Sarah unaccountably missing. Unwilling to spoil the tête-à-tête which Charlotte, amazingly, appeared to be relishing, Arabella looked about for Joseph. She caught a glimpse of him talking earnestly to Captain Desormais and made her way towards them. She was just about to interrupt their conversation when something about the stout figure rang a warning bell. That hair—short, the curls artistically disarranged—was not Joseph's.

A chill shiver trembled through her as she realized how nearly she had committed the unforgivable error of forcing her company on the Prince of Wales. The resemblance to Joseph was even greater now that they wore similar clothes, but she doubted whether such an excuse would have proved popular.

As she hesitated, a laughing voice sounded behind her: "Alone, Miss Ridware, no partner? May I beg the honor of the next dance?"

She spun around.

"Tom! Whatever are you doing here?"

"Now come, Arabella, that's scarcely a polite greeting."

"Mr. Knighton . . ."

"I prefer Tom," he murmured sadly.

Her lips twitched but she repressed her amusement and refused to respond to the disturbing smile.

"How did you get here? You cannot have been invited."

"I have to own that our host omitted to send me an invitation card but I decided to forgive his oversight and come without."

"Shameless!"

"Not at all. Merely resourceful. I am glad to see that you have honored my poor flowers."

"So they *were* from you . . ." she bit off the words, sorry to have betrayed so much.

"Who else? I thought it only fair," he added audaciously, "I noticed how you begrudged poor Grace hers that day."

Arabella's eyes flashed angrily for a second but weakly she allowed his warm smile to melt her rage.

"You are too kind, Mr. Knighton."

"Then you will repay me with a dance?"

She could feel the curious eyes on them but did not care. Awkward questions might come later but she was determined to enjoy the moment. Perhaps Sarah might be too intent on forwarding the match between Charlotte and Sir Giles to worry about her.

In a pleasant euphoria, she allowed Tom to lead her on to the floor. Acutely aware of his hand upon her arm she gazed happily up at him. Tom was very distinguished this evening in his beautifully cut coat. How had he come by such a garment? Impossible to achieve such a perfect fit unless the garment had been made specially for him but how could an ordinary smuggler afford such a luxury?

With a sudden surge of inner laughter she wondered what the polite people around them would say if they knew just who—and what—Tom was. Not that it was easy even for her to credit it, but what did it matter. She would savor this moment while the madness lasted.

It was the supper dance. As it finished, Tom led her into the refreshment room and heaped her plate with dainties. She surveyed the impressive display approvingly.

"What a tremendous variety. No wonder they needed Monsieur Dubois."

Tom raised an inquiring eyebrow and she explained:

"Our chef. We lent him to the Prince to help prepare this gargantuan spread."

"Really! I am suitably impressed. I had not realized you were on such intimate terms with royalty."

"Don't scoff! I didn't mean to brag. Captain Desormais arranged it all."

"Did he suggest it?" Tom's voice was suddenly serious.

"Not exactly. Sarah offered but he had been giving some very broad hints. Why?"

"No matter. I was merely curious. Do you know that repulsive child in pink who is waving in this direction?"

"Lord, yes! It's Charlotte—and Sir Giles. I hope she doesn't bring him over, I can't abide his groping fingers."

"Then let us make our escape while we may."

He threaded a way through the crowd and pushed open one of the great doors that led on to the terrace. Arabella followed gratefully breathing in the cool air.

"What a relief to be out of those grossly overheated rooms!"

"True. Our royal host does keep his home infernally warm."

"My host, not yours. Tom—why did you come here tonight?"

"To see if you would wear my flowers. Why else?"

"Be serious!"

"I am serious, Arabella," he took her hand and she trembled as he gazed so unsettlingly down at her. "Please believe me. I wish I could take you fully into my confidence but the secret is not mine. Can you trust me?"

Gazing up into those steady grey eyes, she nodded breathlessly.

"Yes, but Tom—how long before you can explain?"

"Not much longer, I hope."

"I hate to see you run such risks—like coming here tonight."

"Who'd know me? Even if they had seen me in the village they'd imagine themselves mistaken."

"But the smuggling. I fear for you there, and for Edward too. He seems determined to embroil himself in your activities."

"I know it. I try to discourage him but it is hard to put off such a high-spirited boy. He is bound to find some form of mischief if his father persists in keeping him tamely at home. You cannot tie him to your apron string for ever, Arabella."

"I don't wish to—but you will look after him, Tom?"

"I'll do my best."

"And you'll take care yourself?"

"How can I refuse when . . ." he broke off suddenly as another door opened further along the terrace. A stout figure in dark blue coat, walked out and peered around him.

"It looks as if Prinny has a secret assignation," murmured Tom.

They watched him move out on to the terrace. His huge silver buttons glittered in the moonlight. Beside her in the shadows, Arabella felt Tom tense with anticipation. She stared anxiously not knowing what to expect but sure that something was about to happen.

Sure enough as the plump figure looked about him three men sprang from the shadow of a clump of shrubs and knocked him to the ground.

"Tom! The Prince! Help him!" shrieked Arabella. When her companion made no move, she turned angrily, only to discover him helpless with mirth.

"The bungling idiots! They've got the wrong one."

She looked again at the struggling group and realized that once more she had confused Joseph with the Prince.

A bald head shining in the moonlight proclaimed that

this was her brother struggling valiantly against the attackers.

"Well even if it is only Joseph, we must help before they murder him," she exclaimed indignantly.

But before they could move, Joseph had grabbed the smallest of his assailants and dragged off the muffler that hid his face.

"Dubois!" he boomed incredulously.

As the deep voice rang out the other two men stepped back in sudden doubt.

"Mon dieu! Ce n'est pas le Prince!" gasped the little chef.

The door behind Joseph opened once again and Captain Desormais stood sternly regarding the struggle. Dubois with a sudden twist freed himself and ran off, closely followed by his two companions. Captain Desormais glared furiously after them then bent to aid their victim.

"If Your Royal Highness injured . . ." he asked deferentially, then in utter amazement:

"Mr. Ridware!"

Joseph sat up weakly, rubbing his shoulder.

"Desormais, what the devil is going on? Those fellows jumped out on me."

Arabella shook off Tom's hand and ran across.

"Are you hurt Joseph?"

"Hurt, of course I'm hurt, girl! That damned scoundrel Dubois knocked me down. The man's a maniac! Last time any foreigner sets foot in my house—don't mean you of course, Desormais," he added belatedly.

Arabella's lips twitched. Obviously Joseph was recovering.

"Are you feeling well enough to come back inside?"

"Of course I am!" He rubbed his head ruefully and realized that his wig was missing. He felt around for it then pushed it back on to his head.

"I cannot understand why that French lunatic should assault me."

"They thought you were the Prince, Joseph. Didn't you hear Monsieur Dubois say so?"

"Thought I was the Prince! You're madder than Dubois, Arabella."

"I fear, Mr. Ridware, that your sister is correct," put in Captain Desormais gravely. "You were undoubtedly the victim of an attempt to capture the Prince of Wales. Bonaparte would pay well for such a valuable hostage."

"Then you mean that Dubois was a spy," breathed Arabella in sudden horrified comprehension.

"I fear so."

"My God—and I sent him to the Pavilion!" groaned Joseph.

"But you did not know he was a spy, Joseph."

"Who will believe that?"

"I think, Mr. Ridware, that by yourself falling victim to his attack, you clear yourself of any complicity in his plot, though I do not understand what you were doing wandering out here alone."

"I was looking for Arabella. Charlotte had some foolish tale of seeing her go on to the terrace with a strange man . . ." He broke off with an embarrassed cough as he realized that such an explanation was scarcely tactful.

"All nonsense, of course," he added unconvincingly.

Captain Desormais fixed a cold gaze on Arabella's flushed countenance.

"You *were* outside Arabella! With whom?"

10

Arabella stared into Captain Desormais' accusing face, her mind a horrified blank. She cast a quick glance back along the terrace. Thank goodness, Tom had vanished! With him gone there was a chance that she could conceal his part in this misadventure.

"I—it—was so terribly hot in the supper room I thought I would faint so I stepped outside for a breath of air."

"With whom?" repeated the Frenchman coldly.

"On my own!" She refused to meet his sternly incredulous gaze.

"I thought that I saw you earlier with that tall fellow from the village—the fisherman. You are sure he was not with you?"

This contemptuous reference to Tom infuriated Arabella and the sudden spurt of anger gave her the courage to fight back. What right had Captain Desormais to question her thus? She would resent such an accusation from Joseph and he was her legal guardian. The Frenchman had no claim on her. They were not engaged yet— nor would they ever be if Henri continued to make himself this offensive.

"Nonsense! How do you suppose such a person could come here? Do be sensible, Henri."

He relaxed slightly as he appreciated the logic of this.

"I beg your pardon for doubting you, Arabella. My concern for you made me too suspicious. I am delighted to hear that I was mistaken. That fellow is deeply involved in this unhappy business and I should hate to see you entangled with him."

Miserably Arabella wondered if he spoke the truth. Could Tom have known in advance of the plot? What was it he had said as Joseph sprawled on the terrace?

"They've got the wrong one!"

The words surely showed foreknowledge of the attempt. Was that the reason that he had risked coming uninvited to the party at the Pavilion? Dully she had to admit that it sounded a far likelier explanation than his claim to have succumbed to an overpowering desire to see Arabella herself. Tom had never before betrayed any extraordinary interest in her company. She did not want to believe him guilty but the more she questioned, the more the insidious doubts grew.

A door behind them opened cautiously. As they spun around to see who was approaching so secretively, they were amazed to discover the Prince of Wales, creeping stealthily out on to the terrace. He moved eagerly towards Arabella, then, perceiving the two men behind her, turned abruptly and hurried back inside.

Captain Desormais spoke quickly:

"I think, Mr. Ridware, if you are now fully recovered, you should take Arabella back in. I am sure you will not wish your absence to be remarked on."

He hesitated then added confidentially:

"I would be greatly obliged if you both said nothing of this affair—not even to your family. If it became common knowledge it might give rise to unnecessary alarm. I will have a word in private with His Royal Highness to put him on his guard."

Abruptly he left them and hurried after the Prince. Arabella helped Joseph to brush the dust from his clothes.

Joseph twitched his wig straight then led her back into the Pavilion. In the crowded ballroom, Arabella parried Sarah's furious questions abstractedly. She was relieved when, at last, Henri reappeared to claim the dance she had promised earlier. It put a halt to Sarah's probing and gave Arabella time to think.

Henri's manner had changed. The arrogance was gone and he seemed more than ever anxious to please, to re-trieve the position lost by his discourtesy on the terrace.

It was difficult to talk while they danced. Impossible to broach the subject that filled her thoughts. Mechanically she performed the figures but all the time her mind was occupied with Tom. The heat of the room no longer bothered her. She felt numb and cold. In her aching head the same questions pounded over and over. Was Tom a traitor? Why had he come here tonight?

She looked anxiously around the room but Tom's broad-shouldered form was no longer to be seen. He had vanished as mysteriously as he had come.

Afterwards she remembered little of the remainder of the evening. She sat, danced, conversed in a sick daze. When finally they found their wraps, dragged Joseph from the card room and said their adieus, she was vaguely aware of Captain Desormais beside her. He pressed her hand significantly, murmuring:

"Good night, Arabella. I look forward to our meeting tomorrow," then more loudly, "I will wait upon you at noon, Mr. Ridware."

He stepped back to let the yawning footman close the door and put up the steps.

"Did you hear that, Joseph, he must mean to make Arabella an offer at last," exulted Sarah as soon as the door was safely shut. "More than you deserve too, Miss! Running off with that strange young ne'er-do-well. I saw you slip out with him whatever you may pretend. Thank Heaven that Captain Desormais did not suspect your wanton behavior."

Her sister-in-law's waspish voice barely penetrated Arabella's consciousness. She stared ahead with unseeing eyes. Was Tom really a traitor? Desperately she ached to trust him as she had promised but the evidence seemed to pile up so damningly against him.

She knew him to be a smuggler, suspected that he might be a deserter, too, but still she could not accept that he was a traitor. Tom could not be guilty of such a crime. Tom, whose presence filled her with delight; Tom, who exasperated yet entranced her; Tom, whom—she must finally admit it—whom she loved; Tom could not be so base—could he?

To smuggle was dishonest, worse in time of war. Desertion was an uglier fault but treason was a thousand-fold worse. She could not believe Tom to be that evil.

Suddenly she remembered the review. If Tom were false, why had he saved the Prince from assassination? Grimly Henri's words echoed in her mind:

"Bonaparte would pay well for such a valuable hostage."

Desparingly she felt her head would split with the effort of thinking. Nothing was clear to her any more except that, innocent or guilty, she loved Tom. She hugged the knowledge to her, a gleam of comfort in the dim morass of doubt and uncertainty.

The birds were already trilling their dawn chorus before she fell into a restless sleep.

All too soon Mollie was dragging open the bed curtains.

"Wake up, Miss Bella! It's past eleven o'clock already."

"Go away," moaned Arabella drowsily. "I'm tired. I want to go back to sleep."

The covers were ruthlessly tugged off her.

"There's no time to sleep, Miss Bella. Mrs. Joseph says you are to be got up at once. She says that fine French Captain is coming over to see you this morning."

Arabella sat up reluctantly. She stretched wearily and tried to rub the sleep from her tired eyes. Automatically she reached for the cup of steaming chocolate which Mollie brought each morning. The creamy warmth revived her a little. Stifling a yawn, she murmured:

"Captain Desormais coming this morning? Oh yes, I remember now. He did say something last night, but why is Sarah in such a tizzy? If she's up let her entertain him till I'm ready."

"Oh come along do, Miss Bella," scolded Mollie. "Hurry yourself. It's you the Captain wants to see! Mrs. Joseph is sure he means to make you an offer today. You cannot keep him waiting at such a time!"

In her shock Arabella swallowed a great gulp of the hot chocolate and choked as it burned its way down her throat.

"An offer," she gasped as soon as she had sufficient breath. "Oh no, she must be mistaken!"

Not now, she thought wildly, not after all the confusion last night. She had to have time to sort out her feelings.

"Come now, Miss Bella. You must have noticed how very particular the Captain's manner has been of late. You should have hinted him off if you wasn't ready for a declaration."

"Too late to tell me that now," responded Arabella gloomily.

Realizing that it was pointless to delay the inevitable, she roused herself, washed quickly, then stood resignedly while Mollie brushed her copper curls.

Not until the older woman fetched a new striped gown from the closet did she try any protest. Then:

"Mollie I cannot wear that! It looks so calculating. As if I was hanging out for an offer—all decked out to impress."

"Now don't be mulish, Miss Bella. This is the gown Mrs. Joseph says you was to wear. I'll be the one to suffer if you go down in anything else."

"And you so terrified of Mrs. Joseph," said Arabella with heavy sarcasm. "Oh very well! Just to keep the peace."

She fidgeted impatiently as Mollie tied the narrow ribbons beneath the high-waisted bodice.

"Well, have you finished yet? Is the lamb ready for the slaughter?"

Mollie's wrinkled face was troubled.

"Be serious for once, Miss Bella, I beg you. This is a big decision for you to make. The Captain seems a real gentleman for all he's Army not Navy like your poor papa. I don't know where you'll find a better offer. You can't pretend you're always happy here. Mr. Joseph don't understand you like the old master did. Don't give this Captain a hasty answer you'll maybe regret later."

Sobered, Arabella turned and gave her a swift hug.

"I promise I'll be sensible, Mollie."

"May God guide you to make the right decision, Miss Bella."

Tears sparkled in Mollie's eyes as she watched Arabella go downstairs.

In the breakfast room, only Edward lingered. Preoccupied as she was, Arabella could not miss his effervescent mood. She surveyed him dubiously.

"You seem remarkably elated, this morning. What mischief have you been up to?"

He glanced around cautiously then leaned closer.

"I went on a run last night."

"With the smugglers?"

"Not so loud! Anyway, free traders sounds better."

"Free trader or smuggler, they both hang if they're captured," she snapped crossly. "How could you . . ."

As Edward frowned and motioned her to be more quiet, she dropped her voice to a cross whisper.

"To join the smugglers on a run! After you promised me that you would keep out of their activities."

He glared back, equally indignant.

"I did not! I only promised to be careful. I was too!" A mischievous twinkle animated his face. "Just as well we were cautious. Someone had informed again and there were Revenue men all over the place. We'd have been taken, for sure, if we hadn't been on the lookout for trouble. But we spotted them in time and sent the women to deal with them while we slipped past."

"The women! What could they do?"

"Now Bella, use your imagination. What do you suppose they do to take the excisemen's minds off their duty?"

Arabella flushed vividly as she realized what he implied.

"How positively disgraceful!"

"Well the females they chose, ain't precisely ladies, Bella. More Grace's sort. They take a couple of bottles of brandy with them and keep the Preventives happy till the cargo's safely past. By that time, the poor dolts of Excisemen are usually too drunk to be any trouble—not that that kind of woman is particularly fussy about her virtue anyway."

"And their unmaidenly efforts got you all safely away last night?"

"Yes, and the cargo too. Mind you, I had a notion that everything didn't go quite as planned. No one would tell me exactly what was intended—all very secretive— but I got the distinct impression there was something special planned that didn't come off. They all seemed to be in a sweat waiting for something or someone that didn't turn up."

Suddenly Arabella's wandering attention was riveted as her quick brain slotted this tale neatly into the events of the previous night.

"The Prince! That's who they must have been expecting. They'd be going to ship him across to France."

"What are you on about now? Why should Prinny have anything to do with it?"

"He *must* be the one they were expecting! Of course you don't know—some men tried to kidnap him last night but they got Joseph instead."

"Father?"

"Yes. You should have seen Monsieur Dubois' face when he realized his mistake."

"You mean Dubois was mixed up in this?"

"Yes, he was one of the men who attacked Joseph."

Edward's face cleared.

"That accounts for it then. I thought these kidneys were devilishly overdone. Old Hamstall's sister never could cook a kidney."

"Edward! How can you think of your stomach at a time like this? Don't you realize you nearly helped ship the Prince of Wales over to France? You might have been hanged for treason."

"Drawn and quartered too, no doubt," responded Edward cheerfully. "No, Bella, I can't see Sam or Jack lending themselves to a scheme of that sort. They aren't traitors. Nor is Tom—though he wasn't with us last night."

"No he wasn't," snapped Arabella. "He was at the Pavilion making sure the whole thing went off smoothly."

"Tom was? You must be wrong, Bella."

"I assure you that I am not! I was with him when the men jumped out on what we supposed to be the Prince. Then Tom realized it was Joseph."

"What did he say?"

"He laughed! You know he cannot be serious about anything. I had not fully realized what was happening

then. It was not until Captain Desormais mentioned
spies . . ."

"Desormais? Now I could believe him capable of anything. And it was he, remember, who persuaded us to
send Dubois to the Pavilion."

"Your mother made the offer."

"Only after some very broad hints from your fine Captain. Mark my words! It is your precious Henri who is
the traitor. I never did like the fellow—you cannot trust
a man who has no sense of humor."

"No sense of humor! Henri?" exclaimed Arabella.
"What about all those amusing tales? Even you laughed
when he told us about Mr. Brummell and the . . ."

"Oh I grant you he can rattle off any number of droll
stories but he can't take a joke against himself. Remember how annoyed he got when Charlotte would go on
about frogs' legs."

Arabella had to admit him correct. Henri had been
furious at Charlotte's silly comments.

"But that doesn't make him a traitor."

"No, but it all points the same way. That mystery about
Grace, denying he was at Brighton, getting Dubois sent
to the Pavilion."

Arabella was still unconvinced.

"You cannot be serious, Edward. How could Henri be
a French spy. He was brought up in England and has a
job so close to the Prince."

"What better place for a traitor to insinuate himself?"

She shook her head hopelessly, knowing it useless to
argue further with Edward. Once he had made up his
mind about anything, he could be as obstinately immov-
able as his father.

It would certainly be very convenient to believe that
Henri was the villain but it was too easy a solution. The
very strength of her desire to prove Tom innocent, made
her even more suspicious of such a facile theory.

If Tom were guiltless, why had he chosen that particular night to appear at the Pavilion? Surely the coincidence
was too great, especially as he had disappeared again so
swiftly after the abortive attempt to abduct the Prince.

No, however little she relished the conclusion, she had to recognize that Tom was indeed the traitor. What misguided thinking, what disastrous chain of circumstances had led him to this position, she could not guess, but that he was indeed the traitor she was unhappily convinced. Totally oblivious of her dissension, Edward leaned excitedly closer.

"You keep an eye on that Frenchman, Bella. Mamma reckons he is coming here this morning. You watch him and I'll go and tell Tom what we have discovered."

"No, Edward, you must not . . ."

Before she could say more, Sarah had hurried fretfully into the room.

"So this is where you are dawdling, Arabella. Come along at once, child, for Heaven's sake! Captain Desormais is already with your brother."

Arabella ignored Edward's conspiratorial wink and gloomily followed Sarah into the drawing room.

"Here, child, sit on the sofa, and take this piece of fancy work."

She thrust the half-worked stool cover into Arabella's reluctant hands.

"But, Sarah, you know how I hate needlework."

"Never mind that! There is nothing that shows off a lady's hands to better effect than needlework—unless it is the harp, but that would scarcely be appropriate."

Arabella scowled at her, asking tartly:

"Are you sure I should not perform a jig or two, to show off my ankles or breathe deeply to display my bosom to greater advantage?"

"Arabella! I cannot imagine how a girl who has been as carefully reared as you were, could turn out so disgracefully vulgar. Why a gentleman like Captain Desormais bothers with you, I do not know. Still, as he is so misguided, it is my duty to help you achieve a respectable match however little you merit it."

A rebellious answer trembled on Arabella's lips but she thought better of the impulse. Instead, to relieve her feelings she dug the needle viciously into the canvas.

"No! No! Not as if you were using a poker! Every one

of those stitches will have to be reworked. *Là,* Arabella, my sweet, what exquisite taste you show in your choice of colors to be sure."

Sarah's shrill complaint sank to an affectionate coo as a servant announced Captain Desormais.

Before the Frenchman had completed his polite greetings, a giggling Charlotte tumbled in and gabbled off an obviously rehearsed message. Sarah rose.

"I am sure you will excuse me, Captain Desormais. Some little domestic crisis appears to need my presence."

"Allow me to go instead . . ." stammered Arabella, only to subside weakly as Sarah, darting her an angry glare, declared with sugary sweetness:

"No, my dear. I am persuaded that Captain Desormais would greatly perfer your company to mine. Now, Sir, do not be so ungallant as to deny it. Come, Charlotte."

Arabella felt the hot color flood into her cheeks as the door closed behind them. Sarah had not the tact even to wait till Henri requested an interview with Arabella. She was positively throwing her sister-in-law at his head.

Captain Desormais came slowly across the room. Arabella kept her eyes upon the needlework she still clutched. The great uneven stitches that she had set in her fury, seemed to glare out at her and she moved a trembling hand to cover them.

"Arabella!"

She was completely incapable of looking up. Staring fixedly down, she could see only the gleaming toes of Henri's hessians. Did he truly use champagne in his blacking to achieve that glassy finish, she wondered wildly, or was that just one of Edward's silly jokes? The boots moved closer and she forgot about everything but Henri's nearness as his voice came low and more urgent:

"Arabella, you must know why I am here! I have seen your brother. He gives me leave to make my application to you, so you need not be afraid to listen to me."

Indignation at his calm assumption that Joseph's sanction for his suit was more important than her own, dispelled Arabella's bashfulness.

"I am not my brother's chattel, Captain Desormais, to be granted or withheld as he chooses."

"Indeed, Arabella, I did not intend to suggest such a thing. I merely presumed that you could not wish to commit yourself without his approval."

"I am completely capable of making up my own mind."

"And I admire you for it, chérie. It was your independence that first attracted me to you. But let us not protract this interview, Arabella, you must know my feeling towards you. Will you do me the honor of consenting to be my wife?"

Confidently he sat beside her and took both her hands in a warm clasp. Up till that moment she had been uncertain. The advantages of the match were very real—very tempting—but all at once, she knew what her answer must be. Struggling to free her hands, she exclaimed brokenly:

"Captain Desormais—Henri—you mistake my feelings! I cannot marry you—I am not in love with you."

His arm moved around her waist, drawing her close.

"Marry me and the love will come."

She shuddered, suddenly feeling his closeness was oddly menacing. She pulled free from him.

"No! I cannot! Please, Henri, do not persist. It is impossible. I cannot marry you."

For a fearful moment she felt the anger surge through him. She felt wretchedly guilty, wondering whether her careless friendliness had encouraged Henri to fall more deeply in love with her than she had realized. Then she remembered his cold insolence on the terrace and Sir James' coarse words flashed through her mind. It was the loss of her fortune not herself that was proving so agonizing for Henri.

"No, Henri! Do not say any more. I am truly sensible of the compliment you pay me but I cannot accept your offer."

"Arabella, you leave me desolated. Can you not reconsider? Have I perhaps been too precipitate?"

The door opened and Sarah bustled in, beaming at them both.

"Well my children, is it all settled? Let me be the first to congratulate you."

Arabella stared unhappily at her, too miserable even to be cross at the ill-breeding of Sarah's abrupt reappearance. Swift to censure bad manners in others, it was typical of Sarah to be so careless of her own behavior. It was left to the Frenchman to reply frostily:

"I fear, Madame, that your congratulations are not in order. Miss Ridware has not consented to become my wife."

"You cannot mean it, Captain. Arabella cannot have *refused* . . . My dear Captain Desormais, you must be mistaken!"

At any other time, Arabella would have laughed to see how ludicrously quickly the complacent smile faded from Sarah's face.

"Arabella, tell Captain Desormais he has misunderstood you!"

"Captain Desormais has informed you correctly, Sarah. I am deeply sensible of the honor he has paid me but must decline his offer," declared Arabella woodenly.

"Pay no attention to her, Captain Desormais. The silly child is nervous, overwrought! Her brother will speak to her. Have no fear. She will agree," gabbled Sarah desperately.

Captain Desormais bowed coldly.

"I hardly feel, Madame, that I could wish for an unwilling bride!" His eyes softened as he turned back to Arabella. "But, Arabella, if this is indeed only maidenly modesty I will give you time to reconsider."

"Oh yes, yes! She will soon see how foolish she has been," asserted Sarah confidently.

Arabella bit the inside of her cheek firmly. Edward must be right. Henri had no sense of humor. Surely anyone with any sense of the ridiculous could not fail to be diverted by Sarah's desperate attempts to make everything go as she intended. Henri merely ignored her interruption.

"I had regretted that His Royal Highness' decision to return to Carlton House, tomorrow, would separate us as soon. Last night's events really upset him. Perhaps they have overset your nerves too . . ."

"Yes, of course—she is overwrought—doesn't realize what she is saying . . ." twittered Sarah.

Again Henri totally ignored her.

"Perhaps now my absence will prove a good thing. It will give you time to reconsider your decision carefully. No!" He held up a firm hand as Arabella opened her mouth to deny that there could ever be any alteration in her answer, "don't commit yourself now. I will speak to you again when you have given the matter further thought. Your servant, Madame."

With an abrupt bow, he left them, brushing an excited Charlotte out of his path. Charlotte stared after him in fatuous delight before she ran to fling her arms around Arabella.

"Oh, Bella, I'm so happy for you! What did he say? When is the wedding to be?"

"You may well ask," snapped Sarah grimly. A few remaining shreds of good breeding had made her swallow her rage until Captain Desormais left them but now it boiled over.

"That—that wicked girl has just turned down the best offer she is ever likely to have! I wash my hands of her! Obstinate, self-willed hussy, she'll not be satisfied till she has disgraced us all."

With a horrified screech, Charlotte interrupted the tirade:

"You've never turned down Henri, Bella! Are you mad?"

"Demented, undutiful, depraved, what do the words matter? To refuse after all her brother's effort!"

"You had best look out, Bella, or I'll be wed before you. Sir Giles was very attentive last evening. I'd jump at the chance of becoming mistress of that great house of his."

"Think it over carefully, Charlotte. You would be very foolish to marry merely to gain an establishment. Remember you have to put up with Sir Giles too, if you want to rule his household. I call that a poor bargain."

"Pay no heed to her, Charlotte! The silly girl does not know what she is talking of. Wait until your brother hears of this morning's work, Miss. He'll not be too dainty for plain speaking."

At this threat, Arabella's frail control over her temper snapped.

"If it is plain speaking you require, Sarah, let me inform you roundly, that I consider it thoroughly immoral to subject an innocent young girl to be mauled around by Sir Giles Farnham!"

Sarah's voice cut icily through Charlotte's gasp of outraged protest.

"You have grown very nice in your notions all at once, Miss. These views are vastly different from your conduct last night—sneaking off to assignations with strange young men. If it is a connection with that low creature you are hoping for, you can rid your mind of any such nonsense. Your brother will not permit you to disgrace us with any misalliance. Better take the Captain while his offer is still open. It won't be, for much longer, if he learns of your scandalous behavior."

"I will not marry Captain Desormais! Not if it means remaining a spinster all my life," declared Arabella passionately. She slammed the door behind her before Sarah could summon breath to assure her that such would surely be the result of her waywardness.

11

Joseph certainly had a vast deal to say on the subject of Arabella's perversity and ingratitude. Sarah lost little time in pouring the whole tale into Joseph's incredulous ear. Before she was half finished, he was bellowing for the wretched girl to be brought to him.

The summons was hastily delivered by a quivering servant but while Arabella was reluctantly preparing to come downstairs, a message from Sir George Leyton called Joseph out on urgent militia business. Passing his quaking sister in the hall, Joseph commanded her ominously to use the time till his return in thinking over her willful conduct.

If she had hoped that the delay might blunt the edge of Joseph's fury, she was sadly mistaken. In a protracted and painful interview, Joseph castigated her behavior, character, opinions and attitude with a grim thoroughness. He recalled her every misdeed from infancy onward. Each minute detail was resurrected and flourished before her. She would never, thought Arabella resentfully, have imagined Joseph to possess so retentive a memory. Although Joseph undoubtedly exaggerated the crimes, as she listened to his catalogue of the low spots of her seventeen years, she had to admit, with unhappy guilt, that she remembered most of the misdemeanors he described.

In uneasy fascination she watched Joseph's angry complexion progress from pink through scarlet to a livid purple. His peroration mounting to a furious climax, he finally ran out of insults and was reduced to repeating the more acrimonious in a wildly incoherent bellow. But although the details might be obscured, the message came clearly through to her. Joseph demanded that she consent immediately to marry Captain Desormais. White-faced, she defied him.

As his rage grew more ungovernable she was horribly afraid that Joseph would take his strap to her—not for the first time. In the past she had felt its lash only too often in retribution for those crimes he had been recollecting. To her relief Joseph retained sufficient command over himself to know that physical violence would be unavailing. After a last graphic description of the fate she might expect, should she persist in her obstinate refusal to oblige her family, he dismissed her, warning:

"Don't think you can rely on your inheritance to support you, Miss. Father knew your willfulness and tied it safely up. Not a penny piece of it can you touch unless I give leave. If you are still hankering after that fortune-hunting jackanapes who has been sniffing around you, you will see how fast he runs off when he knows you penniless. Then maybe you'll wish this day's work undone."

Escaping from him feeling utterly shattered, Arabella hesitated to return upstairs where she knew Mollie would be waiting eager to know the outcome of the quarrel. She felt unable yet to face the affectionate inquisition.

Her only hope of solitude was the library but even that was not empty. As she slipped in, Edward rose from an armchair.

"I thought you'd come here. I gather that my Papa is not pleased with you."

"An understatement! Do you know what he threatens? To pack me off in disgrace to Great-Aunt Maria's in Yorkshire."

"I'd have thought you'd welcome it. It'd get you out of father's way."

"Great-Aunt Maria's worse! Perhaps you don't remember her last visit. A dreadful old woman with a pack of revolting little pug dogs."

"I remember right enough. One of the little brutes bit me. I must admit, Bella, that on second thoughts I don't think it at all wise to send you there."

"I should think not!"

He shook his head gravely.

"A very unwise suggestion! You might corrupt the poor old dear with your depraved conduct and low propensities!"

"You were listening!"

"I doubt whether anyone in the house could help hearing—with the possible exception of Hamstall's sister who's as deaf as a post. My revered parent has a remarkably carrying voice when he's in a passion. Did you notice that it rises with his color. By the time he reaches that rich magenta hue you can hear him from cellar to attic."

"Charming to know that every servant in the house was able to listen to all the insults he heaped on me," commented Arabella bitterly.

"Cheer up. Some other scandal will come along to take their minds off it soon enough. If it is any consolation, you have my wholehearted approval of your wisdom in turning Desormais down. Father will live to be grateful when he discovers that his fine Captain is a French spy."

"Hush, Edward! You must not say such things. I've told you it is Tom who is the spy not Henri." She paused, unwilling to ask the question yet desperate to know its answer. "Did you see him? What did he say?"

"Who, Henri?" asked Edward teasingly.

"You know who I mean—Tom? What did he say?"

"Nothing. Sam said he'd gone."

"Gone? Where?"

"No one seemed to know for sure but they think he's chased after that flighty piece Grace. How he can want anything to do with her after she tried to get him pressed, I can't for the life of me understand, but Sam reckons that Tom is still besotted with her."

Arabella hoped that her face did not betray the hot surge of jealousy this news caused her. Edward continued:

"Poor Sam is really cut up about it all. Grace went off immediately after that business in Brighton when she sold all her beaux to the press gang but it appears that Tom soon went along to Hove after her and made up their quarrel and he's been seeing her regularly since."

"Hove? I thought she came from Seaford."

"She does but she's made that too hot for her ages ago. She's working with the smugglers at Hove now and a real unpleasant bunch they are. I thought Tom too decent to get involved with such a set of ruffians but Sam says he's thick as thieves with them."

"So you learned no more of last night's affair?"

"Nothing definite but some pretty odd rumors have been floating around, about the smugglers wanting to capture Prinny. Sam's in a rare taking. I told you he was as patriotic as they come. One of Grace's fine friends had arranged it—asked Sam to ship out a smuggler who'd got into difficulties. Sam thinks he wouldn't have discovered who he'd really got till it was too late."

"Who was this friend?"

"No one I've ever heard of—but that proves nothing. Desormais would obviously use a go between."

"I still cannot believe that Henri is involved. Surely Edward, you must admit that Tom's behavior is far more suspicious."

"Then why did Grace and dear Henri try to ship him off to sea?"

She shook her head wearily.

"I don't know! Perhaps some lovers' tiff between Tom and Grace. I'm still not convinced Henri had anything to do with that business."

"To hear you go on anyone would think you liked that French ninny. I suppose you didn't get a chance to sound him out about last night."

"No."

"It's a pity you couldn't have kept him dangling a bit longer. Give us an opportunity to keep a watch on him. Couldn't you pretend you'd changed your mind?"

"Really, Edward, you are disgusting. I have quite sufficient of your papa trying to make me change my mind without you starting too. I will not marry Henri for you or anyone else."

"All right. Hold your horses, Bella. It was just a thought. I didn't expect you to go so far as to marry the fellow, just pretend. I'm not on father's side. Not that he needs help. He'll nag on at you till you're sick of the sound of his voice."

Sarah and Joseph did indeed try all ways to persuade Arabella to change her decision, but their arguments, cajoling, threats were all equally unavailing. Opposition only made Arabella more obdurate, more stubbornly convinced that she had done right to refuse Henri's suit.

Only her mother's distress caused her any regret and to do her justice, Mrs. Ridware did not try to alter Arabella's decision. Too accustomed to be dominated by her forceful daughter, she confined herself to declaring plaintively:

"What I cannot understand, Arabella, is what your objection is to Captain Desormais. He seems such an excellent young man, one of whom your poor dear papa would have thoroughly approved. Sarah tells me that I must insist that you accept his offer but I cannot urge you to marry where your affections are not engaged, although I thought you so well suited. Are you so very adamant, my love?"

This gentle pleading succeeded where all Sarah's recriminations failed, in making Arabella feel guilty, but it was equally ineffective to change her mind.

As the days dragged on, Arabella felt the atmosphere at Ridware Hall grow increasingly hostile. Joseph barely spoke to her now and Sarah confined herself to mournful predictions that they had seen the last of Captain Desormais. When Arabella was driven to declaring that she sincerely hoped that her sister-in-law was correct, Sarah warned:

"Mark my words, Arabella, you'll live to rue the day you threw away this chance."

Charlotte, reveling in the unexpected delights of being ardently sought after, was insufferably smug. Unwisely she attempted to echo her mother's warning and flaunt her own happier condition. Seething, Arabella favored her with her frank opinion of Sir Giles Farnham——his person and morals. Although this annoyed Charlotte it made little real impression on her but the plain speaking so relieved Arabella's feeling that she was afterwards able to endure the revolting spectacle of Sir Giles drooling over Charlotte with resigned tolerance and the distinct satisfaction of knowing that she had done her duty. No one could blame her now, she decided, for whatever disasters followed the seemingly inevitable match.

It was not in Charlotte's nature to bear a grudge so she soon resumed her breathless confidences, owning herself to be in daily expectation of Sir Giles' proposal. Now, however, she was careful not to appear to crow over Arabella.

As October wore on, the weather became bleaker, suiting Arabella's mood. A fortnight of overcast skies with persistent drizzle and sea mists made everyone's thoughts turn with mounting apprehension across the channel to where on the obscured French coast, Bonaparte's forces were reported to be massing more determinedly.

"No one," declared the pessimistic Joseph with gloomy relish, "could hope for more perfect weather for an invasion sortie. The French will be here before the month is out."

His opinion was shared by many others. All but the most heedless kept anxious watch upon the beacons that stood out stark against the grey autumn skies. Day and night, men waited tensely beside them, ready to set them alight and flash the news of invasion from hilltop to hilltop across the whole kingdom.

On her restless rides around the countryside, Arabella saw no sign of Tom. She had to stay content with the rumors that Edward gleaned of Tom's swift progress to leadership of the Hove smugglers.

Sam and Jack, hurt by his abrupt desertion, turned bitterly against their former friend as tales came of his ruthless measures to insure control, ably abetted by Grace. Even Edward, reluctant to believe any ill of his hero, showed signs that his faith in Tom was wavering.

The local smugglers found their activities greatly curtailed by a combination of the loss of Tom's guidance and the greatly increased military and naval activity along the coast. It made them still more resentful of the reputed success of audacious forays by their Hove rivals, led by Tom and Grace.

Having lost one outlet for his energies, Edward flung himself more enthusiastically into his volunteer training—not always in directions most calculated to please his father.

"Any more of your brain-waves and we'll have no one left to drive off the enemy," declared that harassed individual bitterly as he regarded the shambles that resulted when Edward persuaded his fellow volunteers to try out his scheme for a novel cavalry charge. Its toll amounted to four men, incapacitated with fractured arms and cracked ribs, and two horses. One with a strained fetlock would recover eventually, the other sustained a broken leg and had to be shot. Its owner was heard to regret that a similar fate was not meted out to Edward, advising Joseph:

"The best thing you can do with that lad, Mr. Ridware, is to ship him off to France. He'll do more good to our cause fighting with Boney than upsetting us all here."

The prospect of Henri's return was constantly in Arabella's thought, looming blackly on her horizon. She was thankful when in mid-November Joseph hurried home with news of the Prince of Wales' return to Brighton. Against the express wishes of the Prime Minister, he reported, the Prince had insisted on returning to lead his regiment.

Captain Desormais had come with him and had found time to send word that he would wait upon them shortly. Arabella greeted this news with relief. She would be glad to give Henri his final answer and relieve the tension in the household.

Many sleepless nights had not altered her decision. She knew herself to be in love with Tom whatever his faults. In time she might overcome the weakness but until then, she must stay single. There was no hope of marriage with Tom but marriage with anyone else was unthinkable.

Disgrace and banishment from Ridware Hall might

follow her refusal but at least she would know the whole matter was over and done with.

As Arabella let out her involuntary sigh of relief at Joseph's news, Sarah glared disapprovingly. Totally ignoring the presence of Sir Giles, come, yet again, to dine with them, she axclaimed:

"Now, Arabella, I trust when Captain Desormais arrives, you will do the right thing and oblige your family by agreeing to this match we have so carefully arranged for you."

Arabella scowled as she retorted angrily:

"I am sure, Sarah, that Sir Giles is not interested in our private family affairs."

"Don't fret yourself about Sir Giles. I count him as one of the family already."

"Your dear sister-in-law is perfectly correct, Miss Arabella," Sir Giles seized the opportunity to emphasize his point by squeezing her knee. Quickly she moved out of range of the groping fingers. Catching the movement, Edward declared dulcetly:

"Very true, Mamma. I've noticed Sir Giles to have a great feeling for the family. Has he not, Bella?"

Bestowing a quelling glance on the baronet as he edged closer, Arabella agreed tartly:

"I've always found Sir Giles *touchingly* familiar."

Unruffled Sir Giles shifted his attention to the more responsive, if less tempting, Charlotte, who giggled up at him in coy delight as he slyly pinched her. Sarah watched this by-play with fond complacence.

From the hall came six silvery notes as the clock chimed the hour. Everyone looked expectantly at the door but no Hamstall appeared. As the minutes ticked past, Joseph drew out his gold hunter and with a frown checked the time. He snapped it shut declaring crossly:

"It is past six o'clock! Why is dinner late? I will not tolerate unpunctuality."

As he spoke the door opened. Joseph started impatiently to his feet.

"At last, Hamstall! What has been keeping you?"

Strangely white-faced, the butler hesitated in the doorway. He gulped then, with a great effort, disciplined his face to its habitual wooden passivity as he announced:

"Dinner is served, Sir, and word has come that the beacons are lit."

12

Seven pairs of eyes stared blankly at the butler.

It can't be true, was Arabella's first coherent thought. For months they had waited for the invasion, discussed it, made elaborate plans for what they would do when it occurred but now that it was actually upon them she realized that she had never truly believed that it would come. She had known that the French might attack but unconsciously she had assumed that they would choose some distant part of the coast—not here!

Hamstall's news shocked her and she reacted in hurt disbelief. Then, seeing his scared white face, she recognized that it was true. The French had come. All at once her personal problems seemed insignificant, compared with this great catastrophe.

A quick glance at Joseph showed him equally flabbergasted. Rooted to the spot, he licked dry lips, quavering:

"Are—are you sure, Hamstall?"

Edward was the first to move. He ran to the window and dragged back the heavy brocade curtains. An angry red glow filled the room, dimming the light of the candles.

"By Gad, he's right!"

The lurid reflection shone red on Edward's face, already flushed with excitement.

There was a soft thud as Sarah slipped senseless to the floor. Mrs. Ridware moved to tend her. Unexpectedly she was the calmest of them all though Arabella realized that she should have anticipated this.

"After all," Mrs. Ridware had once told her daughter when they were discussing the possibility of an invasion, "when your poor dear papa died, the worst thing possible happened for me. So long as you are safe, my love, I have no fear of the French."

Charlotte started up, terror stricken, as the ominous

140

red light pervaded the room. Her face quivered and she began to scream hysterically:

"Boney's coming! He's come to murder us all! I know he is. What shall we do?"

Sir Giles pushed her gently back into her chair and patted her comfortingly.

"Now, now, Miss Charlotte. You're quite safe with us."

Contemptuously Arabella noted that, even now, his greedy hands seized the opportunity to grope and squeeze.

"Hurry, Father! The volunteers will be assembling, already." Edward rounded impatiently on his father and Joseph, recovering from his stupefaction, roared out a stream of conflicting orders:

"Fetch Wyrley! Tell him to lay out my uniform at once! Have the carriage brought around! Tell all the volunteers to leave whatever they are doing and assemble on the lawn! Where's my horse? Has Sir George sent word? Why is everyone just standing there?"

"Papa," shrieking Charlotte ran and clung to him. "You cannot leave us, Papa! I won't let you. Who will protect us from the French?"

"Nonsense, girl." Joseph was slowly recovering his composure. "We settled all this a long time ago. I have to go and drive the devils back into the sea—or at least win time enough for you to ride away to safety. Now where has that boy got to—Edward! Time we were away."

He scurried out after his son.

"I won't go on that nasty horse. I won't! I won't! It's cold and dark out there," Charlotte shrieked.

"Be quiet, Charlotte!" Arabella stepped across and slapped her sharply.

Sir Giles muttered in protest but the sobs ceased abruptly. Charlotte put a surprised hand to her cheek where a scarlet imprint of five fingers showed the force of the blow. Firmly Arabella insisted:

"Now, Charlotte, you know there isn't room for us in the carriage. You'll be perfectly safe with me. Go straight upstairs and put on your riding dress as quickly as you can."

"I'm too frightened," whimpered Charlotte.

"There is a spare seat in my gig. May I offer it to the young ladies?" put in Sir Giles eagerly. He leered across at Arabella. "It will be a bit of a squeeze but I'm sure none of us will mind that in an emergency."

Arabella shuddered, feeling that, if given the choice, she would infinitely rather take her chance with the French than be squashed up in a gig next to Sir Giles for hours.

"Thank you, but no. We need to preserve as many horses as possible from the enemy. Come along, Charlotte!"

Her face blotchy with weeping, Charlotte still protested obstinately:

"No, I want to go with Sir Giles. Please, Mamma, say that I may."

Sarah had regained her senses by now and was more than ready to seize any chance to further her match making hopes.

"Yes, of course you may, my dear. Take Betsy with you if Arabella is too ungracious to accept Sir Giles' kind offer. Come Fanny! We must rouse the children and be away as swiftly as we can. How thoughtless of the French to choose such a thoroughly inconvenient time to invade us!"

Realizing that it would be hopeless to protest further, Arabella hurried upstairs to don her own riding clothes, dismissing her maid's help.

"I can manage, thank you, Mollie. Go and get yourself ready to leave and make sure that Mamma gets into the carriage safely."

When she came back downstairs, Edward thrust a packet into her hand.

"Here, take this, Bella. You'll be hungry before the night's out. They're all at sixes and sevens in the kitchen but I grabbed what I could. Good luck!"

Arabella took it dumbly. At present even the thought of food choked her but she appreciated Edward's thoughtfulness. It would be a long time before she reached Richmond and by then hunger might have overtaken the sick excitement that now filled her.

Outside, Joseph was already mounted. His horse's chestnut flanks gleamed in the ruddy light, which was slowly fading now as the beacon fires burned lower. From along the carriage drive she could hear the excited babble of the grooms and footmen who had been sent on ahead.

With a pang of regret she watched Edward mount and follow his father, the two ridiculous helmets jogging away after their troops. Before they were completely swallowed up in the darkness Edward turned and shouted:

"You'll have to go saddle your mare yourself, Bella. Old Bilston can't cope in the stables."

Then they were gone. Arabella stared after them, her eyes fogged with tears. Would she ever see them again? She bit her lip resolutely. It was no use to think such gloomy thoughts. Whenever she had imagined the invasion she had pictured herself as calm and heroic. It was daunting to realize how scared and alone she felt.

As she approached the stable yard, Sir Giles' groom drove out his master's gig. Bilston, grumbling fiercely, was attempting to harness the team to the coach with the aid of the sole remaining stable boy—an undersized twelve-year-old.

"No one thinks how we'm supposed to manage out here with all my lads off as soldiers. I'm too old and rheumaticy for this sort of caper. Miss Bella, that's a fact."

She did her best to help, trying to remember the complicated arrangement of traces and poles. If this was to become a regular task for her, she would have to study the art.

Eventually the great coach was ready to move out. Creaking, Bilston climbed up on to the box. The stable boy moved across to the stall where Arabella's mare stamped fretfully, but Arabella stopped him.

"No, leave her, Abel. You'd best go with Bilston. Mrs. Ridware will need your help to load up the carriage."

As the heavy coach rumbled out of the yard she felt horribly alone in the dim stables. She pulled down her saddle and flung it across the mare's back. She must hurry! No one would think to wait for her in all this confusion and she did not relish the prospect of a lonely ride in the darkness with the French liable to be waiting around any corner. Her trembling fingers slipped on the buckles and the mare, catching her panic, snorted and kicked. Arabella forced herself to be calm, to work slowly and carefully, to forget all those horrid stories people related ghoulishly of French brutality.

When, at last, she rode around the front of the house, a distracted Sarah was superintending the loading of her silver into the boxes on the coach roof, ignoring Charlotte's frenzied demands to leave it all.

"I am not leaving my best plate for any French scoundrel to make off with!"

The children, frightened at being wakened so abruptly and dragged from their warm beds out into the chilly darkness, were crying dismally. It was no wonder they were terrified, thought Arabella sympathetically, with Bonaparte held out to them so long as an awful threat, an ogre who flourished on an exclusive diet of naughty children.

Arabella's mother, clutching the tapestry bag that contained a few treasured remembrances of her late husband, tried to comfort them, and gradually their noisy sobs faded to a whimper.

"Stop that whining at once or Boney will come and take you off," snapped Sarah, undoing all her good work and they howled in earnest once more.

At long last the little cavalcade moved off. Arabella fell into place behind the carriage, Sir Giles' pair prancing nervously behind her. With no pretensions to being blood cattle, they had, nevertheless, sensed the fear in the air and reacted to it as temperamentally as any thoroughbreds. Their alarm communicated itself to Arabella's mare, which sidled and danced uneasily as they were held up at the lodge gates, while two farm carts lumbered past. A huddle of sleepy children perched on top of the piled up furniture and goods. Clearly the whole neighborhood was on the move.

Once the carts were past, Bilston drove out. There was no room to pass in the narrow lane so they were forced to creep along behind the lurching carts, catching up more and more slow moving vehicles till they crawled in a great sluggish stream of traffic. The confusion reminded Arabella of their journey to the review, only now, instead of being choked with dust and heat, they shivered, in the cold night air, through a thick sea of mud.

Fretful at their slow pace, Arabella envied the riders who sped past in the misty darkness. Some frantically pressed inland; others, in hastily pulled on uniforms, galloped purposefully against the tide of traffic, down towards the coast. Frantic voices hailed them as they passed, but they would not slacken their pace to answer any question. Perhaps, thought Arabella dully, they knew as little as anyone else of what was going on.

There was a confused shouting in the distance and the cart in front of them stopped abruptly. Bilston pulled his team to a halt and Arabella moved prudently aside as a cursing Sir Giles wrenched his headstrong pair to a standstill not far short of the coach's rear.

Sarah poked her head out of the window.

"What's going on? Why have we stopped?"

The panic evident in her voice set the children wailing once more and Sarah shouted more sharply:

"Move on at once, Bilston! We cannot afford to loiter here."

"If you knows how to drive these here cattle through two farm carts, a chaise and a wagon, you'm welcome to try it, Ma'am."

Hardly heeding his words, Sarah shrieked over the noise of the children's crying:

"Don't be obstinate, Bilston! Do as I say, immediately!"

"T'aint no manner o' use getting all hoity-toity, Ma'am. I'm adoing my best. I can't work no miracles."

"Wretched man! This is the last time you drive me anywhere. My husband will dismiss you instantly, when he hears of your insolence."

"If that's what you wants, Ma'am, I'll leave here and now."

Bilston tossed the reins into the hands of the stable boy and prepared to climb down off the box. Arabella hurried forward to act as peacemaker.

"Please don't be hasty, Bilston. Mrs. Joseph is upset by all the worry. She did not really intend to dismiss you. Do, please, stay with us, if only for the sake of my Mamma and the poor children!"

Muttering sullenly, he allowed himself to be persuaded and snatched back the reins from his vastly relieved companion.

"Very well, Miss Bella. I'll bide for the sake of the little ones but don't go expecting no miracles!"

"Thank you, Bilston. I'll ride ahead and see if I can discover what is causing the hold up."

Once she had led her mare along the grassy verge past the line of stationary vehicles, it was easy to see what was producing the confusion.

An overturned cart blocked the roadway. In their panic to escape the French invaders, people had obviously dragged out any available means of transport and the strain had proved too great for this dilapidated cart. One wheel had sheered off, causing the overloaded body to tip on its side, and prevent the passage of any other vehicle. Its owner stood wringing his hands beside it, hopelessly surveying his widely scattered belongings, while the drivers of the following vehicles clustered around, shouting at him to move his wreckage or vainly trying to manhandle the clumsy obstruction from their path.

A troop of dragoons, splendid in their gold-laced jackets, jogged towards the disturbance. The officer halted his men just short of the wreckage.

"What is going on here?"

Everyone tried to explain at once.

"Silence!"

The incisive command cut through their babble.

"There is no need for this panic, my good people. The enemy have not landed."

"But the beacons—the signal?" protested a dozen voices.

"A false alarm. The French are not come. It is perfectly safe for you all to go back to your own homes."

There was a buzz of relieved chatter and scattered cheering as his report spread back along the line of vehicles. By the time Arabella pushed her way back to rejoin her family, the news had already reached them.

"Do you think it is really true, Bella?" quavered Charlotte fearfully. "Or is it another trick to deliver us all into Boney's hands?"

"Of course it is true, you goose! I heard the dragoon major himself say that the whole affair was a false alarm."

"Then why aren't we moving?" demanded Sarah.

"There's an overturned cart blocking the road, further up. The dragoons are trying to right it but it will take them some time. Perhaps Bilston can turn the carriage," she ignored his aggrieved mutter of protest. "See, Bilston, someone has opened a gate over there. You can drive into the pasture and turn there."

There was a frenzied confusion as the carts and carriages tried to crowd through the narrow gateway. Feeling her mare tremble again, Arabella called:

"I'll move out of the way. You'll probably catch me up soon but if not I'll see you at home."

As she coaxed the mare around, a rider bumped into them. A flicker of light from the flares held high to enable a cart to safely negotiate the gateway, shone momentarily on his face. He turned away instantly but the glimpse had been sufficient for Arabella to recognize Monsieur Dubois.

What was the Frenchman doing here? Nothing had been heard of him since the unsuccessful attempt to carry off the Prince of Wales. Presumably the rumor of a French landing must have tempted him from his hiding place.

She looked quickly back along the lane at the dragoons but they were all dismounted, trying to right the overturned cart. By the time she had attracted their attention and explained, Dubois would be gone. She must follow him herself. When she had discovered his hiding place, then she could summon help.

Cautiously she started after him. He was pressing his horse but the poor creature was clearly tiring and it was not difficult to keep him in sight. It was harder to persuade her mare to move silently along the uneven grass bank so that the chink of metal hooves on the loose stones on the road would not warn the rider in front that he was being followed.

She hesitated as he branched down a muddy lane. This was well off her route home but she could not bear to lose her quarry now.

The trees of the hedgerow crowded in more closely here. Their tops branched over to make a roof across the lane. Though the fallen leaves that once clothed them lay in a soggy carpet underfoot, it was still dark and eerie beneath the bare branches. She started nervously as an owl hooted above her, then anxiously peered into the gloom ahead. Where was Dubois?

As she paused irresolutely, a hand seized her bridle and desparingly she stared down into the mouth of his pistol. She had not been as skillful as she imagined. The Frenchman had set an ambush and now had her captive.

"Eh bien, Mademoiselle! It is you who are so inquisitive. *Quelle dommage!* I have no desire to harm so charming a lady but I cannot have you betray me. Are you alone?"

Haughtily she met his searching gaze. She was terrified but determined not to let him know it.

"No! Mr. Edward is following just behind me with more assistance."

He smiled unpleasantly.

"You lie, Mademoiselle. Your Edward is off with those stupid volunteers. You forget I was forced to join their ranks myself so know their duties."

She glared mutinously at him refusing to let him see the fear that trembled through her.

Dubois remounted and motioned with the pistol.

"Ride on slowly, Miss Ridware. No tricks mind, or I'll have to shoot you. I don't want to do so but I will if you force me, never fear."

Recognizing that he spoke the truth, she obeyed. She wished despairingly that she had not yielded to that crazy impulse to follow him. Where was he taking her? She was already well off her way home. No one would dream of searching for her here.

At last, at the gate of a tumbledown cottage, Dubois stopped and motioned her to dismount, then cautiously slid off his own horse. He slapped her mare viciously across the rump and the frightened creature set off back along the lane at a gallop.

"There, she will find her way home and they will decide you have been thrown but *hélas,* no one will discover where the so nosey Miss Ridware has got to. Open the gate!"

She was obliged to obey him. As she fumbled with the latch, a dog dashed out of the darkness at them. Arabella cringed back but Dubois thrust her impatiently on. The dog's chain brought him up just short of them and he could only snarl and growl frustratedly at them as they walked cautiously past him.

The cottage door opened a fraction and Grace's dark head peered out.

"Jacques? Who's that you've got with you?"

"That damned girl from the Hall. The silly bitch followed me."

"Why bring her here, you fool?"

"I couldn't leave her lying there in the middle of the lane, could I? Hurry up and let us in."

"He won't be pleased when he hears," warned Grace. "He's in a filthy temper already because you're so late."

Dully Arabella prayed that it was not Tom of whom she spoke. It was one thing to fear Tom a traitor but quite another to see her suspicions confirmed. How could she bear to face him, knowing that all along he had lied to her?

Monsieur Dubois thrust her forward and she stumbled across the threshold into a dirty hallway. Above her a crisp voice snapped:

"What's the delay? Jacques. Grace, why are you dawdling there?"

From the top of the steep flight of stairs, Captain Desormais stared down at her.

"So, Arabella," he smiled silkily, "how kind of you to call."

Arabella forgot the danger and discomfort of her situation as a great weight slipped from her. Jubilantly she cried.

"So Edward was right! It *is* you who are the traitor, not Tom."

"Don't call me traitor, *chérie,* I am a patriot—a French patriot. Do you really imagine that the great Bonaparte would employ such scum as that stupid fisherman?"

Her heart sang so that it was an effort to speak calmly.

"So Tom is not involved in your plots."

"Not in the least. The fool tried to interfere but we soon dealt with him. He is safely occupied at Hove while we work here. Now, Jacques, bring her into the parlor. Grace, see to their horses."

"I set hers loose. It ran off like a thing possessed."

"Imbecile! Suppose anyone sees it. Too late to apologize now. What news do you bring?"

There was a quick exchange in French too rapid for Arabella to follow. She caught odd words but could make no sense of the whole. They kept mentioning *"notre invasion."*

"So it was you who fired the beacons!"

"Moi-même, chérie, and now I enjoy the uproar while your stupid Englishmen dash around the countryside thinking their precious land is threatened. Idiots! There will be no warning when Bonaparte really comes."

"All that confusion just for your amusement?"

"Not precisely. It was what we needed for our other plan."

"Which was?"

Grace had returned in time to hear this.

"Don't tell her, Henri! Least said, soonest mended."

"You worry too much, my dear Grace. Miss Ridware will not be able to tell anyone what she learns. I have a fancy to take her back to France with me. Such a fastidious young creature! Perhaps she'll be glad to agree to marry me after I've finished with her."

His eyes flickered over Arabella's dismayed face with a derisive sneer and suddenly she knew that this was the true Henri—the reality beneath the veneer of charm. With that superficial gloss stripped away, Henri was vicious and utterly ruthless.

"Why trouble to marry her?" Grace laughed coarsely. "You can have all the sport you want without."

"Ah but you forget, *chérie,* that Miss Ridware has a great deal of money and stands to inherit more. When our little ploy succeeds, I am confident Bonaparte will be only too glad to grant her husband leave to keep that wealth."

"I guessed that money was all you were ever interested in," burst out Arabella contemptuously. By fanning her anger she was able to keep those disquieting fears at bay.

"You do less than justice to your charms, my dear, but I grant that the money was equally attractive. I had to find an heiress. You were the best looking and your fool of a brother was busy thrusting you at my head."

"I am glad that Sir James warned me in time."

"So it was that tipsy fool Lengton who scared you off was it?" he said softly. "I'll remember that. He may go whistle for his damned money when I return. I'll not waste your gold, nor Bonaparte's, on such a drunken blabbermouth."

"For what do you imagine Bonaparte will reward you? Your precious invasion scare is a failure. People already know it to be false."

"But in the confusion, no one will be surprised when that fat coward in the Pavilion runs off. Everyone expects him to scurry away at the first hint of trouble."

"You mean to try to capture the Prince?"

"His Royal Wideness? Yes, indeed."

"You won't find it so easy!"

"Oh he'll come running fast enough. I'll tell him his father is run quite demented at the rumor of invasion— for all I know, the old lunatic may indeed have done so —and that the government wish him to hasten to London to be proclaimed regent."

"And what harm can you do him there?"

"That is the touch of genius, *chérie,* I explain to him that the roads are blocked with hordes of stupid peasants and that therefore the authorities consider that to travel by ship would be faster and surer. Then, we sail for France and, *voilà,* a valuable hostage for Bonaparte to bargain with."

It sounded horribly credible but Arabella protested staunchly:

"You'll never get away with it! He'll suspect a trick."

"Not he! With his tongue hanging out for that regency he'll swallow it hook, line and sinker. We've a nice little frigate hovering off the coast not far off, captured a month ago from your Navy. Nothing can go wrong!"

"How could you turn traitor, Henri, after all you told us of your gratitude to the British for sheltering you from the terror?"

His face darkened with anger. His voice shook.

"Gratitude? Can you imagine what it feels like to be patronized, mocked, despised, made the butt of foolish jokes? The British looked down on me as an underling—I who come from the greatest nation in the world."

"Yet you accept their aid and then turn traitor."

"Traitor? To that fat fool in the Pavilion? How can one betray such carrion? I am a patriot—loyal to France and Bonaparte."

He stopped abruptly as the dog outside barked and crashed his chain. Dubois too, listened intently.

"There's someone out there, Henri."

"Help!" Arabella tried to scream but the sound was stifled as Henri's hand pressed viciously over her mouth. She bit savagely. He cursed and twisted a scarf to gag her. His pistol poked into her ribs.

"Quiet! Here, Grace, watch her. Come Jacques! We'll deal with this intruder whoever he is."

Cautiously they slipped out. Arabella listened tensely to the sound of a struggle.

To her disappointment, Captain Desormais came back first. Dubois followed pushing before him a familiar tall figure—Tom!

She half rose but Grace thrust her back into her chair. With satisfaction, Arabella noted that Dubois' eye was rapidly swelling and Henri was rubbing his wrist. Things had not gone all their way though Henri's voice was jubilant as he declared:

"What is your English saying, Arabella? Talk of the

devil? Here is our gallant fisherman. I thought, Grace, that you told me you had him safely occupied at Hove."

"She did her best to dupe me but I'm not so gullible as she imagined. I'm sorry, Arabella, that I could not rescue you. Are you generous enough to take the will for the deed?"

Arabella was conscious of a curious lightening of her despair. Somehow things seemed far less hostile with Tom here, too. She still felt frightened but not so horribly alone. While they were busy tying Tom's hands behind him to the chair rail, she tugged off her gag.

"Tom, they mean to abduct the Prince. To take him to France as a hostage."

"I feared as much but it will do them no good. Boney will never get his army across the channel."

"Channel? We'll hop over that little ditch whenever we wish." Desormais flicked him contemptuously across one cheek. "I cannot waste any more time on this simpleton. Jacques, be sure and have Miss Ridware on the beach at midnight, ready to leave with us. No meddling with her, mind. She's mine—I want the fun of breaking her."

"What about me, Henri? Aren't you taking me too?" shrilled Grace jealously.

"Not this trip, my dear. Two's company, but I'll soon be back for you when Bonaparte leads us into England. Till then you have your fisherfriend there to amuse yourself with."

"But, Henri, you promised," wailed Grace, catching hold of his arm. He shook her off.

"Don't forget, Jacques! Midnight! We must not miss the tide."

Dubois ushered him out. They heard the chain crash as the dog strained to reach him. Tom looked across to where Grace watched them, pistol in hand.

"That's the last you'll see of your French lover, Grace. Why not get even with him by letting us go before Dubois returns?"

"Shut up!" Grace threatened him with the pistol.

"My mother is rich," Arabella tried to speak calmly, "she'd be willing to pay you well if you release us."

"Me, help a silly undersized little bitch who wants to steal both my men! Not me!" Grace came closer and slapped Arabella's face spitefully. "I'll give you what you deserve, you little trollop!" Her eyes gleamed and she raised the pistol taking deliberate aim. "Perhaps I'll shoot you now, before Jacques returns. I'll tell him you tried to escape. Who'll know any different?"

"No, Grace!" Tom struggled desperately against his bonds but before Grace could carry out her threat, the dog's barking heralded Dubois's return.

"What the devil do you think you are doing, wench! Give me that pistol. There'll be hell to pay if we don't do exactly as Henri bids."

Sullenly she let him take it away from her.

Weak with relief, Arabella relaxed. She looked past Dubois at the tiny window and her eyes widened in startled disbelief.

Had she really for a brief moment seen the pale face peering in through the grimy pane or was her imagination playing tricks. She stared again but the darkness beyond the window was blank and empty. Yet she was almost certain that she had really seen that face looking in at them.

13

"What's the matter with that damned girl, now? What's she staring at?" exclaimed Grace sharply.

Arabella reacted quickly. If she had indeed seen someone outside—it would never do to betray his presence to their captors.

Tension made it all too easy to throw real panic into her voice as she shrieked:

"There's a mouse under that window! Get rid of it! I tell you I won't stay here with a nasty creature like that running loose."

Monsieur Dubois sniggered contemptuously, not even troubling to look where she pointed.

"Mouse! You'll have more than mice to contend with before this night's out, Mademoiselle. Henri's hot for you, old lecher that he is. I can't see why he bothers myself. I like a woman to have some meat on her." He tweaked Grace's well rounded rear to prove his point. She flounced crossly away.

"Stop it, Jacques! Henri's only interested in her because she turned her genteel little nose up at him. A bit of opposition always sharpens a man's appetite."

"I can't imagine how you came by that information," put in Arabella disdainfully, wanting to keep their attention away from the window at all cost. "I'd have thought you the sort of drab to fall into the nearest ditch with any man who offered."

Dubois sniggered.

"She has you weighed up, Grace."

"I'll wipe the sneer off her face, the insolent little vixen!"

Grace jerked painfully at Arabella's hair. Dubois pulled her away.

"Now, Grace, don't go damaging the goods. That isn't

155

the way to get Henri back. He'll soon tire of Miss High-and-Mighty when he's had his little bit of sport."

As the tears of pain cleared from Arabella's eyes, she caught another glimpse of the shadowy face peering in through the window. So she had not imagined it. Edward *was* there watching them through the dusty pane.

She froze as Dubois broke off to listen intently.

"Did you hear that noise, Grace? I swear there's some-one else outside."

"With that brute of a dog out there. Never! He'd be kicking up the devil's own racket if anyone set a foot in the garden. You're getting edgy, Jacques. Calm down."

He hesitated, still dissatisfied, then shrugged.

"Perhaps you're right. Who wouldn't be edgy, stuck in this damned hovel for weeks on end? Tonight was the first time I'd been out for a fortnight. I'll be glad when I'm safely back in France."

"You'll never get away with this ridiculous plot," said Tom deliberately. "Why not give up now? You'll get a free pardon if you turn King's Evidence."

"King's Evidence," Dubois spat contemptuously. "That's a laugh. It's the King's son we're after."

"The Prince won't be deceived by Henri's lies," urged Arabella. "After his narrow escape last time you tried to capture him he'll be doubly on his guard."

"You don't imagine Henri told him about that, do you?" jeered the Frenchman. "He kidded the old goat that the highborn lady he was expecting to meet on the terrace had cold feet in case her husband found out, and he easily kept you and your brother silent."

"Then why did the Prince go back to Carlton House?"

"Some scaremonger in London convinced him that it was unsafe here but Henri soon persuaded him it was all a plot to keep him out of the public eye and got the vain fool posting down here again."

Out of the corner of her eye, Arabella saw the door handle move slowly. Grace and Dubois were facing away from the door but at any moment one of them might turn. What could she do to insure their attention was kept away from that direction?

She screamed shrilly, pointing at the window.

"That mouse! I saw it again. Get rid of the horrid thing!"

Startled, Grace and Dubois spun around, following the direction of her outstretched finger. While they gaped, Tom kicked up violently, knocking the pistol from the Frenchman's slackened grasp. It clattered across the stone floor to the far corner. Arabella grabbed frantically at Grace's skirt as the girl moved to retrieve the fallen weapon. There was a ripping sound as the material gave under the strain and Grace jerked free but, by then, Edward was poised in the doorway, a pistol in each hand.

"Keep still, both of you. Bella, for Heaven's sake, get out of the line of fire! I don't want to shoot you after all the trouble we've had to rescue you!"

"Edward," she exclaimed, her knees weak with relief. "I'm so pleased to see you, but however did you find me here?"

She moved across to unfasten Tom.

"Father sent me after you when we discovered the invasion was a hoax. I saw your mare wandering around riderless and thought you'd been thrown. Then I met up with Tom and he told me what was going on. He'd seen you taken into the cottage and he—hurry up and get him free, Bella! If you can't undo those knots find a knife or something to cut the rope. I've got this pair safely covered."

Arabella rummaged through the table drawer and found a carving knife. It was sadly blunt but she sawed desperately at the thick cords with it.

"Take it gently, my love, I'm attached to my hands." Tom's teasing voice calmed her, though for a moment the knife slipped perilously as she realized what he had called her.

"What I cannot understand, Edward," Tom continued easily, "is how you got past that vicious brute outside, so quietly. He nearly had the leg off me."

Edward grinned broadly.

"Easy! I fed him Bella's supper. The poor creature was ravenous. He's my friend for life now. Good job it wasn't

Charlotte I'd given the food to. She'd have bolted that lot herself, before she was halfway down the drive, then we'd have been sunk. Not," he added reflectively, "that it would signify. I doubt if I'd bother to rescue Charlotte anyway. Where has she . . ."

"Edward!"

Arabella's anguished cry was not reproach but warning as she saw Monsieur Dubois leap across and seize the fallen pistol. Before his hand could close around it, Edward had fired and, as the fumes cleared, they saw the Frenchman crouched on the floor nursing his shattered arm.

"Good lad," called Tom.

"Next time I'll shoot to kill," warned Edward cheerfully. "Pick up that pistol, Bella. Then for goodness sake get Tom free Before Desormais comes back!"

"He won't be coming back. He's gone to . . ." She broke off in horror as she remembered just what Henri intended. "Edward! He's gone to abduct the Prince—to take him to Bonaparte."

"Calm down, Bella—and keep cutting."

She tugged at the last cord and it parted. Thankfully Tom stretched and rubbed the circulation back into his cramped arms.

"We've got to find a way to stop Henri," cried Arabella impatiently.

"How can you?" jeered Grace. "It's too late to stop him now. You don't know where the ship is."

"Do you?"

"Yes, but don't think you can get it out of me."

"Why? Has Desormais been so faithful a lover that you cannot betray him?" asked Tom softly. "I thought it was Miss Ridware that he planned to take to France with him, not you."

Grace's dark eyes flashed angrily but she made no reply.

"Don't waste time on her, Tom. I'll warrant our little froggy friend here will be much more obliging."

Edward approached the groaning prostrate figure and stirred it with a careless toe. Waving the pistol suggestively, he demanded:

"Now, Dubois. Are you going to tell us where this ship is or do I have to shoot again? Perhaps I can manage to be a little more accurate this time. Don't watch, Bella, if you don't fancy the sight of blood!"

"No! No! Don't shoot. I'll tell you everything you want to know!" shrieked the Frenchman. He could hardly blurt out the details fast enough and by the fury with which Grace greeted his words, they judged that he was speaking the truth.

Quickly Tom took charge.

"It's about half an hour since Desormais left. He'll be at the Pavilion before I can reach him so I'd best try to intercept him on the way to the beach."

"At the top of that steep rise," put in Edward eagerly. "That's the ideal spot. We can . . ."

"Not you, Edward. You'll have to stay here and look after Arabella."

"And miss all the fun!"

"I'm sorry but we cannot leave her alone here, with this pair."

"You are not leaving me anywhere," declared Arabella firmly. "I'll feel far safer away from this place. Who knows what other cut throats may be lurking about outside. And I suspect," she added darkly, "that there really is a mouse!"

"In that case, my love, we must certainly remove you from such a perilous spot."

Tom's laughing glance made her heart churn once more. Again he had used that casual endearment. Did he really mean it or was it as carefree as the rest of his manner? Already his mind was concentrated on other things.

"Have we any horses?"

Edward considered briefly.

"There's mine and Bella's and I saw a couple in the stables behind here. They're sorry looking nags but I reckon that one should support your weight."

"Good! Now tie that whining wretch to a chair. We'll send someone to fetch him later. We'll take Grace with us, where we can see what mischief she's up to."

Grace cursed him venomously.

"Keep a civil tongue in your head, woman," he commanded in icier tones than Arabella had ever heard him use before.

"Can't you see when you're beaten?" went on Tom, wearily. "The Frenchman was using you and now that your usefulness is over, he has cast you off. All his promises were worthless. You heard him say that he intended to marry Miss Ridware for her fortune, didn't you?"

Doubt showed plain in Grace's scowling face but she was not ready to admit him right. Sullenly she allowed herself to be led out to the stable.

"There's no side-saddle here," reported Edward. "Bella has her own but what about Grace?"

"Never mind that. Grace isn't too bashful to show her legs. I've seen her sit astride a horse before now."

Grace glowered at him but obediently hitched up her skirt and swung astride the pony.

"Keep a good eye to her, Edward," warned Tom, "I'll look after Arabella."

"Don't worry about Grace. I'll put a bullet in her quick enough if she tries any of her tricks."

Twenty minutes brisk riding brought them to the place where the road from Brighton rose steeply to the summit of a fair-sized hill. Just short of the brow, trees clustered thickly at the road edge. Beside them Tom halted.

"This is the perfect place to stop the carriage. The coachman will have his hands full with the horses."

"What sport!" Edward's eyes shone with delight. "Do you mean to dash out with your pistol cocked like a highwayman?"

"As long as there is no guard aboard the carriage with his blunderbuss equally ready," said Arabella depressingly. "Isn't there any other way to stop them?" Then, a sudden memory of the confusion caused by that overturned cart earlier on, gave her an idea.

"Why don't we block the road?" she exclaimed. "There are plenty of fallen branches here. We could drag some of them across the road. Then the coach will have to stop to clear them without you running any risk."

"Good girl!"

She glowed in the warmth of Tom's approving smile.

"Come on, Edward," he called, "help me pull these across. Arabella can watch Grace."

Soon they were regarding with satisfaction the two enormous branches which completely obstructed the way.

"Excellent!" declared Tom. "They won't be able to get past those in a hurry. Now, are you both clear about what you have to do?"

Edward nodded eagerly. Arabella, less enthusiastic, replied:

"I'm to stand out of the way in those trees and keep Grace quiet—shoot her if she tries to give a warning."

"You're sure you could do it?"

Tom sounded concerned as if he sensed her hesitation.

Arabella looked at the sulky black-haired girl and remembered Jem's despair as he was led away by the press gang; remembered Tom's pale weakness as he staggered into the coach to escape the same gang.

"Yes, I could," she declared with utter conviction.

"That's my girl!"

Tom's hand squeezed hers briefly and her heart skipped another beat. How could she ever have believed him false?

"Hush, now, that's the carriage coming now," whispered Edward as the distant rumble and clatter of a vehicle moving swiftly came clearly through the night air. "They must be in a devilish hurry to push the horses so hard on a slope like this."

"Are you sure this is the right one?" breathed Arabella.

"No," admitted Tom soberly, "but we cannot afford to miss. Better to stop the wrong carriage than let Desormais slip by with the Prince."

The coachman's whip cracked and around the bend swayed a light carriage drawn by six sweating horses. With a shout of alarm, the coachman pulled them up just short of the barricade. The postilion swung off the leader and went to investigate the obstruction.

The chaise window clattered down and Captain Desormais' dark head pushed out.

"What's happening, coachman? Why have we stopped?"

"Fallen tree, your honor. We can't get by it."

"Then clear it away immediately and be quick about it. You back there, get down and lend a hand!"

The window snapped shut. A grumbling footman clambered down and began to help the postilion to tug aside the heavy branches.

Large and menacing in the darkness, Tom rode out into the center of the road.

"Stand quite still both of you!"

In the flickering light of the carriage lamps his pistol glittered ominously.

Seeing that Tom's attention was focused on the men below, the coachman reached stealthily for the blunderbuss beneath his feet. From behind him Edward shouted:

"Drop that, coachman! We have you surrounded."

Tom moved swiftly to wrench open the chaise door. Captain Desormais. eyes glittering with baffled fury, scowled at him.

"Knighton! How the devil did you get here?" He recovered swiftly.

"I always knew you for a scoundrel. Have you added highway robbery to your vices now?"

Tom looked past him to where the portly heir to the throne gaped in glassy-eyed amazement at this sudden intrusion.

"I beg Your Highness' pardon but we were forced to halt your chaise. This man intends to deliver you to Bonaparte."

"Nonsense!" A very faint slurring of the sibilants betrayed that Captain Desormais had taken the precaution of priming his royal captive amply before they embarked on their journey. No one could claim that His Royal Highness was drunk but his senses were not as alert as normal.

"Nonsense!" he repeated a little more loudly. "Desormais is our trusted friend. He is taking us to London to be invested as Regent. Must hurry before those damned politicians change their minds again. Drive on coachman!"

Captain Desormais smiled triumphantly.

"You see, Knighton. No one credits your foolish tale. Move out of the way, or do you intend to murder His

Royal Highness with that weapon you are flourishing so dangerously?"

The Prince of Wales frowned and declared unsteadily:

"Put that away, fellow. Don't you know it is treason to threaten your Regent?"

Unnoticed the postilion crept around behind Tom and seized his pistol hand, wrenching it up into the air. Taken by surprise Tom's finger tightened on the trigger. The ball shot harmlessly over the carriage roof.

"Well done!" Captain Desormais climbed jubilantly down from the chaise. "Now we have you, Master Fisherman. Is that you skulking in the shadows, Edward? Drop your weapon and come out or I'll shoot your friend."

Reluctantly Edward obeyed. Arabella pressed more closely into the shadows, frowning a warning at Grace. Henri had not yet suspected their presence.

"Please listen to us, Your Royal Highness," begged Tom. "Don't you consider it suspicious that this man wishes to take you to London by ship? He means your destination to be France."

"How can you expect His Royal Highness to believe a scoundrel who threatens him with firearms?" asked Captain Desormais contemptuously.

"I carried them to protect him from you, Desormais."

"And what evidence do you offer to substantiate your wild accusations?" asked the Prince. He nodded triumphantly as Tom shook his head despairingly. "None! My friend, Desormais, has warned me of the enemy's guile. It is you who wish to betray your Regent, not he."

Henri smirked exultantly at Tom's frustration.

"Move aside, Knighton. Don't you know when you are beaten?"

Impulsively Arabella ran forward.

"Don't trust Captain Desormais, Your Royal Highness. We don't ask you to do anything, go anywhere—just return to Brighton where you will be safe."

"And lose the chance of your Regency!" put in Henri quickly. "Don't listen to Miss Ridware. She is besotted with that scoundrel, Knighton, and will tell any lie to aid him."

In her haste to help Tom, Arabella had forgotten that she was supposed to be guarding Grace and now the dark-haired girl strode forward.

"Henri . . ." she began urgently.

Captain Desormais spun around. Startled to see her there he not unnaturally jumped to the wrong explanation for her presence and exclaimed bitterly:

"Here's another of the shameless trollops! And what do you accuse me of, you lying jade?"

As Grace flushed and glared furiously at him he realized his error but it was too late.

"Lying jade is it?" she echoed softly. "You are the one that lies, Henri, and I can prove it."

"No Grace, I didn't mean it!" he shouted desperately but she would not listen.

"They warned me that you would spurn me now my usefulness is over. Is this how I am repaid for my loyalty?"

"Listen to me, Grace! I did not mean . . ."

She stared stonily at his anguish and turned to the Prince.

"Look in his coat. You'll find your proof there. Letters to his French masters."

At a nod from the Prince, the postilion released Tom and grabbed the protesting Frenchman. He held him fast while Tom drew out a thick wad of papers from inside his coat and handed them to the Prince who ripped them open.

In the dim light they watched his face slowly whiten. Sobered by the shock he swallowed convulsively, quavering:

"My God! It's true! Here's plans of our defenses, letters to the French, lists of agents . . . And to think that I trusted you, Desormais, trusted you implicitly!" He put a trembling hand to his forehead and sat back, eyes closed.

Henri wrenched himself free from the postilion's grasp and made to run off into the darkness. There was a deafening report as the coachman fired his blunderbuss.

The running figure, elegant even in flight, pitched forward and lay writhing in the mud.

"Henri," Grace screamed. She ran to sink on her knees beside him, sobbing: "What have I done? I did not bring them here Henri, I swear it. Jacques told them where to find you, not me."

Captain Desormais lifted a weak hand to press hers then it slipped back and he lay still. Only Grace's noisy weeping broke the shocked silence.

Somehow Arabella found herself clasped to Tom's chest, her face pressed into his coat, trying to shut out the horrible sight.

"Is—is he dead?"

"I fear so, my love, but perhaps he preferred it that way. It was quicker than a long drawn out trial and execution."

"Poor Henri!"

"He knew the penalty for his acts."

"True, and he tried to put the blame on you. Oh, Tom, can you ever forgive me for doubting you?"

Grey eyes smiled tenderly down at her.

"Doubting me? I saw no sign of doubt, though you had every reason to doubt me, my love."

"I believed in you when you were there with me, but I had so many wicked doubts when I was alone. Do you truly forgive me?"

In answer Tom bent to kiss her lovingly. She clung to him, forgetting all the terrors of the night in the comfort of his closeness. At last reluctantly he set her from him.

"I hate to leave you my love, but I must clear up this dreadful business. Edward will take you safely home. I'll come tomorrow to explain and ask your brother for your hand in the approved fashion."

She smiled up at him with the faintest note of regret: "What a thoroughly inappropriate time to propose!"

Dancing grey eyes laughed back.

"I know it but I cannot wait a moment longer. You will marry me, Arabella?"

She nodded, too full of emotion to speak. With a brief hard kiss he let her go.

"Take good care of her, Edward. Till tomorrow, Arabella."

Arabella rode home in a state of weary contentment, oblivious of Edward's chatter beside her. Tom loved her and wanted to marry her. That was all that mattered. She refused to think, tonight, of Joseph's horror when the fisherman came to ask his permission or Sarah's scorn. Whatever they said or did, Arabella was determined to marry Tom.

As they neared Ridware Hall and saw lights flickering through house and grounds, she grew more apprehensive. It was dreadfully late now. How could she explain to Sarah what had delayed her?

"Do you think it is us they're searching for?"

"Maybe," said Edward, adding cheerfully, "Why worry about a little thing like that? You'll have a much worse problem when Tom turns up tomorrow."

"Oh Edward, do you imagine that Joseph will turn him away?"

"He's bound to. Can you see him introducing Tom to his snooty friends—'and this is my brother-in-law, Tom, he leads the local smugglers'?"

"Don't be so horrid, Edward! I though you liked Tom!"

"I do but that doesn't mean I think Father will share my good taste. No, Bella, I'm afraid you'll just have to run off to Gretna Green."

As it turned out, Sarah barely commented on their late return. She was too concerned over Charlotte's continued absence to worry about Arabella.

Thankfully Arabella tumbled into bed. She wanted to lie and think over the night's marvels, but, with a last cheerful thought, that, at least, if they packed her off up to Great-Aunt Maria in Yorkshire, she would be a great deal closer to Gretna Green, which would be a distinct saving on travel charges, she fell asleep.

14

When she awoke Arabella could not, for a moment, remember why she felt so contented. As she lay drowsily savoring the sensation of complete well-being the memory of the night's events burst back into her consciousness. Tom loved her and was coming this very morning to ask Joseph's consent to their marriage. Her happiness dimmed a little as she considered that hurdle still to be overcome.

Joseph was too prejudiced, too materialistic to look beyond Tom's superficial appearance to the qualities beneath. Loyalty, manliness, the attributes for which Arabella loved Tom, would weigh little with Joseph against the grave faults of lack of wealth or family connections.

Still, with Joseph's consent or without it, she intended to marry Tom. Even if it meant complete rejection by her family and a life of poverty, she was ready to face both to be with him. The thought of estrangement from her mother was the only possible consequence of her resolve that saddened her. If Joseph withheld her inheritance, then they would be unable to offer Mrs. Ridware the comfortable home to which she was used, but the idea of their becoming her mother's pensioners was unthinkable. Instinctively she knew Tom would agree with that view. At worst Joseph might manage to convince the over-persuadable Mrs. Ridware that it was her duty to cast off her errant daughter. Arabella would be deeply sorry but even that dreadful possibility was not sufficient to turn her from her course. Come what might, Arabella knew that her happiness lay with Tom.

Mollie, bringing in her morning chocolate, blinked to see her young mistress struggling into her most becoming gown.

"My, Miss Bella, you're stirring early this morning. And why, may I ask, are you dressed up so fine?"

167

Impulsively Arabella hugged Mollie, dancing her around.

"Don't scold, Mollie! I felt so happy this morning I wanted to wear my very prettiest gown."

"Give over, Miss Bella, do or you'll have chocolate all down your best muslin and that won't look so fine," scolded Mollie severely. Then relenting, she smiled. "I thought someone must have told you about the man that's come."

"Already! I did not think to see him so early. Where is he?"

Mollie looked faintly bewildered at her eagerness.

"He's gone of course, Miss. He just left the Prince's message then went."

It was Arabella's turn to look mystified, and a trifle concerned.

"Message! What message?"

"From the Prince, Miss Bella, like I told you. The invitation for you, Mr. and Mrs. Joseph and Master Edward to go to the Pavilion at noon. Mrs. Joseph nearly had a fit when they told her. She says you are to be got ready as quick as can be, so let's get those ribbons straightened out. You've managed to get them into a fine old tangle."

"But I cannot go," cried Arabella in horror. "I am expecting someone else to call this morning. It's terribly important!"

"Well, you'll just have to put them off. When Royalty bids you anywhere it's a command not an invitation like with ordinary folks. You can't refuse."

All her high spirits quenched, Arabella gloomily allowed Mollie to brush her hair and retie her sash and ribbons. Despairingly she reflected that she did not even know where Tom was now to send him a message.

In the breakfast room, Charlotte, even more dejected than Arabella, drooped over her untouched food. She barely responded to Arabella's greeting. Concerned, Arabella asked anxiously:

"Whatever is wrong, Charlotte?"

"Nothing is wrong," snapped Sarah before Charlotte

could make any reply. "Charlotte is a little tired, that's all. The silly child was home very late last night."

"Oh, Bella, Mamma says that I must marry Sir Giles and I don't want to any more. You cannot imagine how horrid he was to me last night—so rough and ungentlemanly—but Mamma insists that I must marry him now." The tears overflowed down Charlotte's cheeks.

Arabella who could imagine his behavior only too well, protested indignantly:

"If you do not like him, Charlotte, then you must refuse to marry him."

"Any young woman who spends the greater part of the night alone with a gentleman is obliged to wed him or forfeit her good name. What Charlotte thought she was about to go off without Betsy I do not know, but as she was so foolish, she must bear the consequences of her rashness. Marry him she must! Not that I consider it any hardship. Sir Giles is an excellent catch."

Cynically Arabella wondered if Sarah would be so adamant to make her marry Tom if she knew that Arabella had spent most of the night in his company—though to be sure they had had Edward as chaperone. Presumably that obviated the necessity. Charlotte seemed unconvinced by her mother's argument too.

"You cannot make me, Mamma. You don't know how unpleasant Sir Giles was last night."

But Sarah had no time for her daughter's misgivings.

"Nonsense, child! I expect he was a little too ardent. You will soon learn to deal with such things, my love. Now remember, when Sir Giles comes this morning I expect you to give him a favorable answer to the offer you say he made last evening. We want none of the silly nonsense we had to suffer from Arabella over Captain Desormais."

Edward, who had arrived in time to hear this, objected immediately:

"But, Mamma! I've already told you that it was a lucky thing Bella did turn down the Captain. He was shot last night in an attempt to abduct the Prince of Wales."

"Maybe he was," responded Sarah coldly, "but if Arabella had not driven the poor man to despair by her shilly-shallying, he might not have been forced to such extremities. Now I cannot stand here gossiping. I have to get myself ready to go to Brighton."

Before any of her hearers had recovered from their shock at such a sweepingly illogical line of argument, she was gone.

"Oh Bella, whatever shall I do?" wailed Charlotte hopelessly.

"Refuse to marry him of course! No one can force you to have him if you do not wish it."

"But Mamma says that if I don't, I'll be utterly disgraced and no one else will ever want to marry me."

"Surely even that is better than having to marry Sir Giles."

"I suppose so, but Mamma will be so cross with me. She won't take me to any parties or balls. I shall have to have Sir Giles after all."

"Lord, Charlie, you don't really mean to make that prosy old bore my brother-in-law do you?"

"I must, though I don't like him anymore. Oh Edward, he was awful! He said such improper things and behaved in such a beastly way!"

"Well, it's your own fault if he did," declared Edward with more candor than tact. "You've been encouraging him for weeks. No wonder he thought you were ripe for a spot of . . ."

"Hush, Edward!" Arabella cut him off as Charlotte began to wail once more. "Now, do be sensible, Charlotte. Crying won't help a scrap. All you have to do is insist that you won't marry Sir Giles."

"But I did so want to be Lady Charlotte and have that lovely house to look after," sobbed Charlotte, "only now I don't like Sir Giles any more."

"Well you can't have the one without the other," declared Edward with brutal frankness.

"Oh, you don't understand!"

Choking her sobs into her handkerchief Charlotte ran out, cannonading in the doorway into her father. Splendid in his newly pressed volunteer uniform, Joseph ignored his daughter's distress as he stared horrified at his son.

"Edward, why are you not dressed? Don't you realize that we are due at Brighton in an hour?"

"But I am dressed and ready, Father."

"Surely you will want to wear your uniform on such an important visit?"

"I can't. It's in a dreadful state after all our adventures last night."

"I asked Wyrley to press it for you when he did mine."

"Maybe but Wyrley won't find the helmet in a hurry. It was so confoundedly in the way that I tossed it over a hedge somewhere."

"Drat it! How can I appear in uniform on my own. I suppose that now I must go and take it all off. I wish, Edward, that you showed a greater sense of pride in your uniform."

Joseph stamped off in a fury.

It was a silent, largely dispirited group who eventually set out for the Pavilion. Joseph was still grumbling about his son's carelessness and worrying whether he should after all have kept on his own uniform. An anxious Sarah fretted lest her daughter should take advantage of her mother's absence to rashly dismiss Sir Giles, thus putting both the girls, whose futures she had assumed to be settled, back on to her hands. Arabella chafed under the necessity of missing Tom's visit. Only Edward whistled cheerfully as they drove off and soon the general gloom lowered even his high spirits.

Two hours later, Arabella positively danced out of the Pavilion. She could scarcely credit that the tall elegant gentleman in naval uniform who had been presented to them by the Prince of Wales himself as "Captain Thomas Knighton" was really Tom, but it was indeed so. There had been no chance to speak to him in the crowded room but an eloquent glance had assured her that, though his circumstances were so altered, Tom's affection was unchanged.

Beside Arabella an equally excited Sarah pressed her arm.

"What a blessing you were so obdurate over that wretched Frenchman, my love! If the engagement had been announced you would have been obliged to wear black gloves for him. So awkward, even though the scandal is to be hushed up."

Arabella was too busy scanning the crowds for Tom's tall figure to pay much heed, though her wandering attention was caught by the next words:

"What do you say to that handsome young officer the Prince presented to us? He appeared vastly épris, my dear, and . . ." Her voice sank to a confidential whisper, "I could not help but overhear that he is the son of Lord Paignton. Only a second son to be sure but his brother is a great deal older and has only two sickly daughters."

Clearly Sarah had not wasted the time they spent waiting among the society ladies for the Prince's arrival. While Arabella had eyes and ears only for Tom, Sarah had been industriously soaking up the tidbits of gossip whispered all around them.

Now with a faintly conscious blush, Arabella asked:

"You mean Captain Knighton?"

"Yes that was the name. No title yet, though with the Prince so interested in him, that may come. Of course it may be years before the Prince is in any position to make good his promises so we must not count on it. Still, Lady Anne Leyton hinted that he has amassed a creditable fortune in prize money so he is already a very eligible party. I think Lady Anne has the notion that he might do for her middle daughter—you know the spotty one."

"I am not interested in Captain Knighton's fortune. I will marry him rich or poor."

Sarah was scandalized.

"My dear Arabella! Not so precipitate. I know that in the past, I have been obliged to hint you to be a little more encouraging but you must not go too far in the other direction. Such want of reticence can only give the young man a disgust of you."

To her astonishment she found that Arabella was no longer listening. Instead she had run across to smile in joyous welcome at the subject of their conversation.

Captain Knighton bent to kiss Arabella's hand.

"At last, Arabella! I thought I should never escape from the crowd inside."

"Are you truly a Captain, Tom? Why did you not tell us?"

"I could not, my love. I was sworn to silence. It was thought that a naval man would find it easy to infiltrate the ring of smugglers who were suspected of plotting to harm the Prince. Not even the Prince himself was told of my identity, because of fears—justified in the event—of there being a traitor among his trusted entourage. Then last night I could not resist the temptation to discover whether you were willing to accept me, poor and wretched as I seemed to be."

"And there was I thinking you were a deserter!"

"That's what you was meant to think, Miss."

With a start of surprise she realized who this broad, clean-shaven sailor, who spoke from just beside Tom, really was.

"You, too, Jack? You really deceived us. Edward thought you completely disillusioned with Tom."

Jack's dark eyes twinkled merrily.

"All acting, Miss. I only wish I could have been in at the finish with you and the Captain, last night."

"We could have done with your help, you old rascal." Edward had hurried over to join them. "I thought at one point that Desormais was going to get away with it. Still it all turned out all right in the end."

"And now you're to join our ship, I hear, Master Edward."

"Yes, indeed! However can I thank you, Tom, for offering to take me aboard?"

"Only by becoming my smartest officer." Tom turned apologetically to Arabella. "I trust that your brother will forgive me for taking the liberty of suggesting such a move to the Prince—and that Edward's mamma will not be too upset."

Strangely enough, Sarah was in favor of the proposal.

"After all," she whispered to Arabella, "it will get Edward out of the clutches of that designing creature,

Sophy Dunster. Did you ever see anything so vulgar as the abandoned way she waved at him when we passed their house, this morning?"

Arabella, who had been privileged to hear Edward's disparaging remarks upon the young lady in question, was about to assure her sister-in-law that there was little to be feared in that quarter, when she realized the error of such a confidence. If his mamma was resigned to his career in the Navy by dread, however mistaken, of his becoming involved with Sophy Dunster, then Edward would scarcely thank Arabella for setting Sarah's fears at rest.

"I agree that it will be the best possible course for him," she said diplomatically. As Tom turned his attention back upon her, she declared. "You see, Tom, already Edward's mamma accepts that it is an excellent plan."

"Yes, indeed—the very best! And he will have the great advantage of being under your care, Captain Knighton!"

"I am glad that you are content to have it so, Mrs. Ridware. You may be sure that I shall keep a good watch over your son. Indeed I must . . ." Though it was Arabella upon whom his teasing grey eyes rested, both ladies were equally delighted by his laughing explanation:

"After all, I am soon to be his uncle now!"